The Weeping Women

Also by Patrick C. Walsh

The Mac Maguire detective mysteries

The Body in the Boot

The Dead Squirrel

The Blackness

23 Cold Cases

Two Dogs

The Match of the Day Murders

The Chancer

The Tiger's Back

The Eight Bench Walk

Stories of the supernatural

13 Ghosts of Winter

The Black Vaults Experiment

All available in Amazon Books

Patrick C. Walsh

The Weeping Women

The third Mac Maguire mystery

Garden City Ink

A Garden City Ink ebook
www.gardencityink.com

A CIP record for this title is available from the British Library
ISBN 9781985000049
Cover art © Patrick S. Walsh 2015
Garden City Ink Design

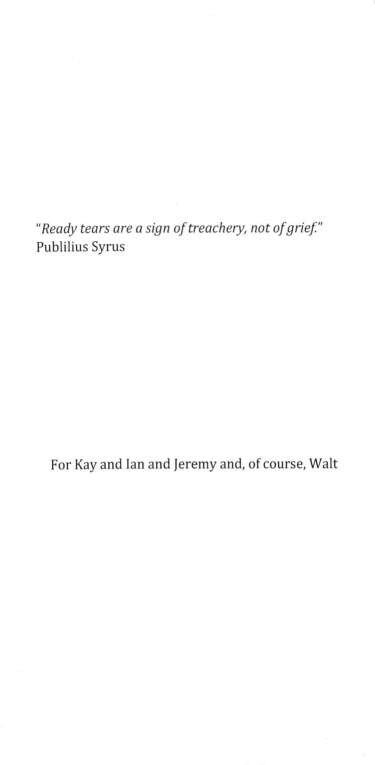

"*Ready tears are a sign of treachery, not of grief.*"
Publilius Syrus

For Kay and Ian and Jeremy and, of course, Walt

Thursday

Mac was once again sitting at table thirteen in the Three Magnets. He was waiting for his friend Tim to return from the bar with some alcoholic refreshments. It had been a slow day for them both so they had decided to take the only rational course of action. They quit work early and headed off to the pub.

He wouldn't stay too long. After a couple of pints and something to eat he thought it quite likely that he'd head for home. He was feeling dog tired so an early night was definitely on the cards. Due to his back pain he'd only been getting three to four hours sleep a night for the last week or so and the deficit was building up. Even Tim had noticed that he was starting to look a bit run down and more than a little fed up.

He gazed aimlessly out of the pub window at the street scene outside. It was just before four o'clock. Lots of people were out and about and the shops were doing good business.

Perhaps it's the sunny weather that's brought them out, Mac thought.

Although it was still only March the sun was shining for the first time in weeks and it was warm enough to allow some of the hardier souls to sit at the outside tables.

Then, on the other side of the window, a young woman sat down. Tears were streaming from her eyes and she looked distraught. Although she was only sitting a few feet away, the glass seemed to somehow make him invisible to her.

She sat near a group of people who were smoking and who seemed totally unaware of her emotional state. They were busy chatting and laughing as the tears raced down her cheeks. No-one took any notice of her.

Only Mac saw her tears.

Chapter One

Friday - nine days before Easter

There were stacks of brightly coloured confectionery on either side of the entrance as Mac walked into the supermarket. This caught him somewhat by surprise. He looked at the displays of Easter eggs and wondered where the winter had gone.

Of course, Easter was going to be early this year so that might explain it, he thought.

He still found it slightly worrying. He just didn't seem to be able to keep track of time the way he used to. When he'd been working his week had been punctuated by weekends off, if he was lucky that is, and there were always monthly and quarterly reports to compile or read. Now the time seemed more like an unending stream and weekends were pretty much the same as every other day.

He sighed. He still missed being a policeman.

He picked up an Easter egg and looked at it. It was the biggest one on display by far. While he'd never had a sweet tooth as such, his wife and daughter had loved the Easter Sunday ritual of smashing several chocolate eggs to bits and wolfing down the contents and he'd loved watching them do it.

He had a sad moment as he realised that he had no-one to buy Easter eggs for any more. His wife had died the year before and his daughter was a woman now and had outgrown childish things. On impulse he put the egg in his trolley anyway, even though he had no clear idea what he was going to do with it.

He continued with the week's shopping. This didn't take him very long. There was just him now and the shopping trolley was far from full. He had just stowed his purchases away in the boot of his old green Nissan when his phone rang.

'Hello, Mac Maguire.'

'Are you the private detective from the website?'

The voice was that of an elderly man and he sounded upset.

'Well, yes I'm a detective alright. How can I help?'

'I'd like you to call around immediately if that's possible. I have a matter of the utmost urgency to discuss.'

'And you are?'

'Montgomery Llewellyn-fforbes with two f's, both lower case,' the man replied. 'Can you come around now?'

Mac agreed and took the man's address. It was in one of the better parts of town, Letchworth Lane near the golf club. Mac hoped that this might be a real case, something he could get his teeth into. He'd not had the sniff of a client for some weeks now and he'd been struggling to find things to do to fill up the time. He went home and stowed away his shopping and then headed towards the golf club.

He pulled up outside a house that he guessed could have happily accommodated a couple of rugby teams and still have had some room to spare. The two-storied building had a gable at each end and a lot of house in between. Mac didn't need to guess that there was money here.

He rang the bell and a crusty old man with a precisely clipped white moustache and a walking stick opened the door. He looked Mac up and down, his eyes lingering on Mac's crutch for quite a while.

'Are you really the detective chappie?' he eventually asked with an inflection of deep scepticism.

'Yes, that's me,' Mac answered already feeling a little annoyed with his prospective client.

'Well, I suppose you'd better come in then,' the old man eventually conceded.

He led Mac down a hallway towards the back of the house and into a large conservatory that overlooked a spacious back garden.

'Here, come and look at what the blackguard did,' he said with some emotion.

He pointed vaguely towards a set of French windows with his walking stick. The doors were wooden and the glass panels were made up of small square panes held in by thin strips of lead. All of the panels were intact.

'I'm sorry but what am I supposed to be looking at?' Mac asked.

The old man went over and had a closer look.

'Oh, she's gone and got it fixed!' the old man said looking a bit put out by this. 'Well anyway that pane there, the one right by the lock, it was broken.'

Mac looked at the door carefully. It had a dead lock.

'I take it that the key was in the lock?' Mac asked.

'Well of course it was. I mean this is Letchworth not one of those heathen places like London. A man should be able to leave his key in his lock without any interference from riff-raff. I can only suppose that this town is finally going to hell in a handcart along with the rest of the country.'

'So, what do you want me to do?' Mac asked.

'Well, catch whoever did it of course. What else? The police aren't interested. They were around here yesterday morning and they said they'd look into it. Not a dicky bird since. Look into it!' the old man said with a snarl. 'They're too bloody busy catching speeding motorists to bother with a real crime.'

He waved his stick around as he spoke and his face had started turning red. Mac hoped that the old man's heart was up to it.

'When did this happen?'

'The night before last and a bloody cheek it was too. We were lucky that we weren't all killed in our beds.'

'What did they steal?' Mac asked, wanting to cut to the chase.

'Why they stole one of the eggs! I'd bought a load of them for the great-grandkids and great-nephews and

4

nieces and so on. I'd stacked them in the living room on top of the dresser and when I came down in the morning little Molly's egg had gone.'

The old man's face spoke of utter shock and horror.

'I'll have to buy another one now, won't I? It was a Peppa Pig one too, they're like gold dust at the moment.'

'Show me,' Mac said his spirits already drooping.

The old man took Mac down a short hallway and then into a spacious room with several studded leather sofas and a wall full of books.

'Just there.'

The old man pointed to a very large Welsh dresser adorned by several framed photographs and stack of Easter eggs.

'Was anything else stolen?' Mac asked.

The old man rummaged around his brain for a moment.

'No.'

'What nothing?' Mac asked incredulously.

'No, we checked and everything was ship-shape and Bristol fashion.'

'So, you rang me because you want me to find whoever it was that stole your Easter egg? Is that right?'

Mac was incredulous.

The old man nodded.

'Yes, that's about the size of it. I want the blighters caught and punished. It's not just the egg it's the damage and the principle of the thing. I'd string them up if it were down to me.'

Mac wondered whether he should just turn around and walk out of the door. However, he'd been so bored lately that he decided on balance that even an Easter egg hunt might be a better alternative to daytime television.

Mac sighed as he told the old man how much he charged. His prospective client gave this some serious thought.

'Very well I'll give you three days,' the old man said. 'That should be more than time enough, if you're a real detective that is.'

Mac silently thanked him for the glowing vote of confidence. He asked the old man a few more questions about the burglary but his answers were far from illuminating. He'd have to see what information the police had on the case.

He gave the house a backward glance as he walked towards his car and shook his head. He wondered if such a surreal episode had really taken place or if he'd just taken too much medication.

He drove straight to Letchworth Police Station and asked for Detective Sergeant Woodgate. He'd only had to wait for a minute or so before Mac heard footsteps coming down the stairs and Toni Woodgate appeared. She was tall and in her late thirties. She was wearing a grey trouser suit and looked as business-like as ever. She smiled and held out a hand to Mac.

'How can I help, Mac?' she asked.

Mac looked around the lobby. There were people around that might hear.

'Can we go somewhere?' Mac asked.

'Sure,' Toni said, mistaking Mac's grumpy expression for one of utter seriousness.

He was grumpy because he really wasn't looking forward to the inevitable embarrassment he'd feel when he told her what had brought him here.

She led Mac towards one of the interview rooms and held the door open for him.

When they were seated she asked, 'So what do you need me for?'

'I've just been hired to look into a burglary,' Mac said.

'Okay, let me have the details,' Toni asked.

He gave Toni his client's name and address. He could feel his face reddening already.

'Yes, that was only the night before last wasn't it? They had an Easter egg stolen.' She stopped and looked at Mac in some disbelief. 'Is that what they've hired you to find?'

'Yes, unfortunately business is slow at the moment and it was either that or Countdown. Can you tell me anything about the case?' Mac asked. 'I couldn't get much sense out of Mr. Llewellyn-fforbes.'

'Well, cases actually,' Toni replied. 'Your client is one of five people in the area who've been broken into and had chocolate items stolen and, as far as we can tell, absolutely nothing else has been taken.'

Mac's embarrassment disappeared when he heard this.

'There've been four other burglaries?'

'Yes. The first one was five nights ago then we had one the night after that and two the night after that one.'

'What's Andy doing about it?' Mac asked.

Detective Inspector Andy Reid was Toni's boss and he'd worked with Mac some years before when they were both part of the London Murder Squad.

'Not a lot really if I'm being honest. He's scheduled to take part in a major counter-terrorism exercise that's taking place in Central London over Easter so we're only concentrating on essential stuff at the moment.'

'And I take it that missing Easter eggs don't fall into that category. Do you think Andy would mind if I looked into these cases?' Mac asked.

'Let's go ask him,' Toni said with a smile.

Mac followed Toni upstairs. She waited for him at the top as he gingerly took it one step at a time. When Andy saw him, he jumped up from behind his desk. He was obviously happy to see his old boss again.

'Mac, how have you been?' he said offering his hand.

Mac shook it firmly.

'Not too bad, apart from being a bit bored I suppose. I'm afraid that business has been a bit on the slow side.'

'How can I help?'

'It's about the Easter egg burglaries,' Toni said helpfully.

'Really?' Andy said as he gave Mac a puzzled look.

'Yes really,' Mac admitted with a grimace. 'Someone's hired me to find their stolen Easter egg. Mac Maguire has officially hit a new low.'

Andy didn't say anything for a moment.

'I wouldn't be so sure about that. I remember when you came to us not long ago about a dead squirrel and look how that turned out. If I'm honest I've been toying with the idea of asking you if you'd look into these burglaries. I've got a feeling that there's more to it than the chocolate but I've no idea why. With this exercise coming up I can't justify expending much resource on these cases but if you're looking into it anyway...'

He thought for a moment.

'Would you be happy to take on all five cases?' Andy asked.

'Absolutely,' Mac replied with a smile.

He was already intrigued. A series of burglaries where only chocolate was stolen was unusual to say the least.

'Toni, can you give Mac a copy of all the files related to the burglaries? I know that you've been hired by someone else but, if anyone asks, you're working for us. Let me know if you find anything.'

'You think that there's something to find?' Mac asked.

Andy looked up at Mac.

'I do. I have a feeling that there's a lot more to this than meets the eye and thanks Mac, it'll be one less thing for me to worry about. Here, you might find this useful.'

He took a warrant card from the desk drawer and passed it to Mac.

'I got the photo from Dan Carter,' Andy explained.

Mac smiled broadly as he put the card in his wallet.

'Thanks Andy. This means more than you'll ever know.'

Toni disappeared for a few minutes and Mac was expecting her to return with an armful of files. Instead she gave him a small memory stick.

'I've put everything on there for you Mac,' Toni said.

He gave Andy and Toni his thanks and left the station with a grin on his face, happy to have something substantial to work on at last. His first reaction on hearing that there had been five break-ins was exactly the same as Andy's.

There had to be a lot more to this than a thief with a sweet tooth.

Chapter Two

He went straight back home, made himself a pot of coffee and started reading the files on his laptop.

He looked at all the surnames of the victims first; Llewellyn-fforbes, Foskett, Pegram, Pratt and Wells. His first instinct was to see if they were all in the same area. He wrote down the addresses. Three of them lived in Letchworth, one in Baldock and the last in Radwell. They were all more or less within three miles of each other. He checked their locations on Google maps but there didn't appear to be any discernible pattern. He topped up his coffee cup and read on.

Mr. Montgomery Llewellyn-fforbes was a retired civil servant who lived in Letchworth Lane, Letchworth. He lived in quite a grand house, one that perhaps might be a good target for any jobbing thief. The thieves got in sometime during the night and made off with just a single Easter egg. Although four people lived in the house no-one heard a thing and the break-in was only discovered the morning after. It was assumed that the thief, or thieves, had climbed over a five-foot high garden fence at the back of the property although no shoe prints or any other evidence was found to support this theory. Mac looked at the photos.

A wooden fence ran along the back of the garden and, although it was hard to tell the scale from the photos, from his visit Mac reckoned that it must be at least a hundred feet long. It was fairly new and it looked in good condition. There was a strip of newly dug ground running right next to the fence. Mac estimated that it would be about three or four feet wide, ready to put some bedding plants in he guessed. On the left of the garden there was a thick hedge, much higher than the fence, while on the right there was an older and slightly higher fence.

Mac looked at the house on Google Earth and he could see why it was assumed that the thief had gotten over the back fence. The house stood on a corner with the main road at the front and a smaller road on the right-hand side. It was surrounded on the other two sides by the golf course. Although it was possible that someone could have gotten over the older fence it was directly overlooked by properties on the other side of the road.

No burglar in his right mind would use that route, Mac thought. It was far too exposed.

The fact that there was nothing else stolen was confirmed by Mr. Llewellyn-fforbes' granddaughter, a twenty six year old doctor who worked at Hertford County Hospital called Helena Biggerstaff. Forensics carried out a cursory examination and found no prints or anything else that proved helpful. Entry had been gained by breaking a small glass pane which allowed the thief to turn the key and open the conservatory door.

The next paragraph was really interesting. No glass had been found inside the house and only a few small shards were found outside. Mac thought back to his meeting with Mr. Llewellyn-fforbes. The flooring in the conservatory was hard, made up of large ceramic tiles.

He tried to picture how it might have been done. He knew that most of the golf course was fenced off but it was so big that parts of its perimeter were unfenced. He also knew that, even where there was fencing, it was sometimes damaged, often on purpose, as some of the locals used the golf course as a short cut at night. So, it would be easy enough for anyone to get onto the course.

The fence at the back of the Llewellyn-fforbes house wasn't that high so it would be easy enough to lower one half of a combination ladder from the other side of the fence so that it was beyond the strip of newly dug soil. It would then resemble a giant step ladder allowing the thief to get easily up and over the fence. Once over a rope attached to the other half of the ladder might then be used to pull it over the fence. The thief could then lay the ladder down flat so it wouldn't be noticed. If the thief knew what he was doing it would take just a matter of minutes.

Mac pictured someone carrying a ladder through the golf course at night in his head. Even if he was spotted by someone, they would probably assume that he was just a workman taking the opportunity to fix some-thing or other while the course was shut.

Once he'd made it to the French windows the thief must have taped the pane of glass up, broke it and then carefully pulled the broken glass out in one piece still attached to the tape. This made for a quieter entry with no pieces of glass falling to the floor or, even more importantly, getting caught underneath the door when it was opened. Due to the tiles, if a chunk of glass had been trapped under the door, it would have made quite a racket when the thief tried to open it. Interestingly the thief must have taken the glass away with him as it wasn't found at the crime scene.

It would seem that it wasn't kids or a random break-in but the work of a real professional. Forensics can get quite a lot of information from a strip of tape but only if it's left behind.

Mac found that he was really interested now.

He read on. There were four people in the house on the night of the burglary; the old man, his grand-daughter Helena and two staff, Freddy and Brenda Michaels. Freddy was the gardener and odd job man while Brenda was the cook and housekeeper.

They all slept upstairs, the family towards one end of the house while the staff had a room at the other end. The conservatory was roughly in the middle. In a house that big it probably would have taken a lot of noise downstairs to wake anyone up but Mac had the feeling that the thief was better than that anyway. There was a burglar alarm fitted but something had gone wrong with it some months before and they'd forgotten to get it fixed.

Mac wondered if the thief knew about this and, if he did, how?

So, all in all, it was a very professional burglary. Mac would wager a good sum of money that the thief was after more than chocolate. But what could it be?

He read the next file.

Marianne Foskett, a retired office administrator who lived in Common View, Letchworth. This burglary took place three nights ago. There were no grand houses here, just Letchworth style cottages and terraced houses. Mrs. Foskett was a sixty eight year old widow who lived alone. She had a big bag of chocolate buttons stolen from her fridge. She'd bought them for her grandchildren who were visiting the next day. It was assumed that the thief came over the fence from an entryway at the back of the property but there was no direct evidence to substantiate this. The thief managed to coax open a kitchen window that probably hadn't been fully shut. Again, the occupant of the house heard nothing. The burglary wasn't noticed until the day after and it was confirmed that nothing else was stolen. There was no burglar alarm system.

He moved onto the next file.

Mr. Robert Pegram, a plasterer by trade who lived in Redbourne Way, Letchworth. This burglary also took place three nights ago. Mr. Pegram's house was on one of the large estates. It was working class and a bit rough, well rough for Letchworth that is. Anyway, rough enough so a burglary wouldn't be totally unexpected. Robert Pegram was a thirty nine year old father of two and a plasterer by trade. He woke up at six thirty in the morning to go to work and noticed that the kitchen door was open and that one of the Easter eggs his mother-in-law had bought for her grandchildren had disappeared. Again, nothing else was reported missing. Mr. Pegram admitted that he and his wife had had a few drinks the night before which might explain why there were no signs of forced entry. Neither of them could remember locking the kitchen door. They had made it easy for the thief who, in all likelihood, had gotten in via the unlocked door after scaling the six-foot high backyard fence from an entryway at the back. Again, there was no burglar alarm fitted.

He moved on.

Next was Miss Alicia Pratt, a twenty three year old bank assistant who lived in Radwell Lane, Radwell. This one took place four nights ago. Radwell was a bit more like Letchworth Lane, nice houses with some being very nice indeed. However, in this case it was a semi-detached house and there was no back fence as a ploughed field lay directly at the rear of the property. As no footprints were found in the field, the investigator assumed that the thief had simply stepped over the three-foot high picket fence at the front of the property and then walked down the path to the kitchen door at the back. This door was locked so some brute force was used to lever it open. Miss Pratt claimed that she was a light sleeper yet she slept right through the burglary. In this case a large bar of Toblerone was stolen. Again, nothing else was touched.

The next bit made Mac sit up. Miss Pratt had a fairly new alarm fitted and it was switched on at the time of the robbery. One of the reasons she'd slept so soundly was due to the fact that her phone line had been cut and, once inside, the thief had levered the alarm box open and disconnected it from the power supply. This confirmed that the thief was indeed a true professional. He would have had only thirty seconds or so to locate and disable the alarm.

He looked at a photo of the alarm box. Its lid had been levered off and he could see that several wires had been snipped. The photos also showed that the box was just a few feet away from the front door so locating it might have been the easy part. Once again, it was a very professional operation.

Finally, Mr. Colin Wells, a builder who lived in Limekiln Road, Baldock. The first of the Great Easter Egg Heists, as Mac was beginning to think of them, took place five nights ago. The photo showed a large bungalow with a drive to the left that appeared to run to the rear of the house. Google Earth confirmed that the drive ended at a garage at the rear of the property. There was a fence at the back and beyond that there was another property so it was unlikely that the thief would have come in that way. Although the driveway had a metal gate, Mr. Wells, a fifty two year old builder, admitted that it was rarely put to use as he kept some of his building materials at the back of the house and he needed to get in and out quite frequently. So, it was likely that the thief had just strolled down the drive from the street and walked to the kitchen door at the back of the bungalow.

Once there the thief gained entry without having to force or damage anything. The investigator asked Mr. Wells if any keys had gone missing but apparently none had. Mac looked at the photo of the door closely then rolled his eyes heavenwards. He had an idea of how it might have been done.

Mr. Wells also mentioned towards the end of the interview that he had two CCTV cameras fitted in the yard at the back because he suspected that's some of the neighbours had been helping themselves to some of his bags of concrete. However, when the investigator and Mr. Wells reviewed the images, all they saw was a static image of a pile of building materials until, one after the other, the screens suddenly went black. When they went outside and looked at the cameras, they found that both had been sprayed with black paint.

When asked what had been stolen Mr. Wells said that a single Easter egg had gone, although the thief had left another fifty-one eggs behind. When asked why he had so many eggs when he had no children, Mr. Wells replied that he'd bought some of the eggs and collected others from friends to bring around the hospitals on Easter Sunday. It was something he'd done for the last six years ever since he'd visited his niece in hospital one year and noticed that quite a few of the children didn't get anything.

With no sign of forced entry, the investigator had asked Mr. Wells if perhaps he'd miscounted his eggs and that perhaps no burglary had actually taken place.

Mr. Wells replied that the egg that was missing was one that he'd bought for his wife. It was a very large egg and it was no longer there. He also stated that his wife had gotten up in the night to go to the toilet and saw someone leaving by the back door. He also said that they weren't in the habit of leaving back doors wide open when they went to bed at night. Mrs. Wells confirmed this but couldn't supply any further details. She said that the person was dressed in black and she only caught the merest of glimpses as he went out of the door.

The investigator had asked about her using the word 'he' but she said it could just have as easily been a woman. The thief wasn't all that tall or short or fat or thin but she added that she couldn't be totally sure on any of these points.

When Mac had finished reading, he topped up his coffee again and gave it some thought. What did he know now that he didn't know before?

The thief is a professional. He accepted the easy opportunities when they came along but could also quickly disable a modern burglar alarm system in seconds if required. He was clean and left nothing behind for forensics to have a go at.

The thief was not after chocolate. If that was all he'd been after then the other fifty eggs in the Wells' house would have also disappeared. He was sure that the thefts were a blind, an attempt to make the break-ins look like a quirky joke of some sort. If that was the case then what was the thief really after? All five victims were sure that nothing else had been stolen so what else might the thief have taken away with him? Perhaps it was information of some sort he was after but what? And why these particular properties? They must have something in common but what?

He wondered if stealing the chocolate was a sort of signature for the thief. Besides the burglars who had a fetish and who would steal women's underwear, shoes and clothes, other mundane things like umbrellas, fruit and music CDs would often disappear too. He remembered that they'd once linked a number of break-ins with a particular music genre, the thief preferring eighties music and especially Abba. Then there was Teabag Tommy as they christened him. He always made himself a cup of tea and even washed up after himself. He was currently doing a nice stretch in Pentonville.

He got Google up and entered 'chocolate thief' as the search term. Most of the results were related to a book of the same name, videos of cute children and reports of actual thefts of chocolate. There was one entry on the third page that Mac couldn't read as it looked like it was in Greek. His computer kindly offered to translate the article for him.

'The Chocolate Thief Strikes again' was the headline. The article was from the month before. Mac was interested and read on.

'The burglar known as the Chocolate Thief has struck again. Two properties in Kolonaki were broken into last night and jewellery, money and other valuables were stolen. A single chocolate bar was also stolen from each property, both Ion bars which are known to be the Chocolate Thief's favourite. Because of the current crime wave due to austerity both houses had alarms fitted but the thief was able to put them both out of action. The robberies weren't reported until the morning after. The thief had been very quiet and the residents of both houses had slept right through the robberies.'

Mac looked up Kolonaki in Wikipedia and found that it was a well-heeled suburb of Athens. He sat back and thought on this. It certainly looked like a similar MO but could a burglar from two thousand miles away really be plying his trade in Letchworth? Of course, the big difference was that, in the Athens burglaries, the thief made off with a sizeable haul while he'd taken nothing other than chocolate from the ones that had been carried out here. It all seemed very unlikely. Mac could only think that it must be a coincidence but nevertheless he made a mental note and filed it away.

He decided that he might as well get on with interviewing the victims. One can only tell so much from photos and statements. He looked at the clock and found that it was nearly four, a good time to start, he thought. Early evening was usually the best time to catch people in.

He decided to start with the first break-in and work his way up to the last one. He rang the Wells' house in Baldock and Mrs. Wells answered. She was happy for Mac to come around and she told him that her husband should be home shortly.

Mac smiled at himself in the hall mirror as he passed by. He was on a case again.

Chapter Three

Mac stood on the street and gazed at the Wells' bungalow. It looked like it might be a pre-war build but it was in excellent condition as you might expect with the owner being a builder. He had a look at the metal gate at the top of the driveway and found that it was held back in place by several bricks. Grass was growing around the bricks so they obviously hadn't been moved for quite a while.

He walked towards the back of the house and noted the positions of the CCTV cameras. One was attached to the side of the house and pointed at roughly forty five degrees to its right, straight at a pile of building materials that took up most of the large back yard. The other was attached to a large shed at the back of the yard. Mac walked over to it. It was also pointed at the pile of concrete bags and bricks but it looked as if it might also include the kitchen door in its field of view.

He could imagine the thief walking down the drive, keeping close to the fence on the left as he came in. Take out the camera on the shed first and then the one on the side of the house. That way he could be sure that he couldn't be caught on camera.

He next went and looked carefully at the kitchen door. It was as he'd thought. He went back to his car and got a broadsheet newspaper out. He'd bought it on the way especially. He slid it slowly underneath the gap at the bottom of the door and then, using a biro, he pushed the key out of the lock so that it landed on the newspaper. He pulled out the paper and the key that had landed on it.

He opened the door with the key and said loudly, 'Mrs. Wells, it's Mac Maguire from the police. I'm at the back door.'

A few seconds later a large woman in her fifties with a puzzle book in her hand waddled down the corridor towards him. She wore glasses and a puzzled expression as Mac showed her his warrant card.

'I could have sworn that I locked that door,' she said. 'After what happened my husband said that we can't be too careful.'

'You did lock the door Mrs. Wells but I got in the same way the thief probably did.'

He explained what he'd done.

'Oh, it's that husband of mine,' she said in an exasperated tone. 'He took the draught excluder off a couple of weeks ago and he hasn't got around to replacing it yet. It's freezing in the kitchen first thing in the morning when I'm doing the breakfast but does he care? I've never heard of anyone doing that before though. Is it something new?'

'No,' he smiled. 'That one's been around since doors and locks were first invented. Anyway, while we wait for your husband, tell me what you saw on the night of the burglary.'

She unfortunately had nothing new to add.

'I notice that you wear glasses. How well do you see without them?' Mac asked.

'Not that well I'm afraid, I'm quite short-sighted,' she explained.

'I take it that you don't put your glasses on when you go to the toilet in the night?'

'Oh no, I'd have to turn the light on and Colin would moan if I did that. He needs his sleep, as he keeps telling me.'

'So, do you think that the reason why you couldn't make out much about the burglar might have due to the fact that you weren't wearing your glasses?' Mac asked.

She took quite a while to think this through.

'Yes, you're probably right. He was all blurry but I forgot that I hadn't got my glasses on.'

'Where exactly did you see him?'

She walked towards the open back door.

'Just here,' she said pointing to a patch of ground just outside the door. 'But it was only for a second. I thought it was some sort of shadow at first.'

'Was he dressed in black do you think?'

There was another silence while the mental wheels turned.

'Yes, yes he could have been but it was so dark outside that I couldn't be that sure.'

The sound of the front door opening caused Mrs. Wells to scurry down the hall.

'Had a good day love?' she enquired solicitously. 'The police are here again about the break in.'

'Really? I thought that they'd given up on us,' a man's gruff voice replied.

The owner of the voice appeared in the hallway. He was a stocky, bluff looking man in his late fifties with a receding hairline and some white straggly bits of white hair sticking out at the side. He wore a pair of stained dungarees over a lumberjack shirt.

'Pleased to meet you,' he said, holding his hand out.

Mac received a firm handshake as he introduced himself.

'He's told me how the burglar got in. Very clever it was too,' Mrs. Wells said.

He took Mr. Wells through it.

He shook his head and said, 'God, that's the oldest trick in the book, isn't it? It's my own fault then for not replacing the excluder. Oh well, it could have all turned out worse I suppose.'

'How's that?' Mac asked.

'Follow me.'

Mac followed the builder into a spacious living room. In a corner there was a massive stack of Easter eggs. There must have been a couple of hundred in there at least.

'Where did all these come from?' Mac asked in wonder.

'It was in the paper, wasn't it?' the builder replied. 'We only had the one egg nicked but when people found out what we were doing they started calling by and dropping eggs off. Well, the kiddies are going to have a bumper Easter this year.'

'Have you had any other thoughts since the burglary? Is there anything that you might have forgotten to tell the police last time?' Mac asked more in hope than expectation.

The builder shook his head.

'What about you, Mrs. Wells?'

He noticed that she glanced at her husband first before saying, 'Sorry dearie but I can't think of anything.'

Mac wondered if there might be something that she wasn't saying. He ran through the names of the other people who had been broken into and asked them if any of them were familiar.

Another shake of the head from the both of them.

'Please just have one more think. Anything, no matter how small or inconsequential, might be important.'

There was silence but Mac noticed the builder's wife glancing at her husband almost as though asking permission. The husband shook his head again.

'No, sorry dearie,' Mrs. Wells said for the both of them.

He left it at that although he made a mental note to talk to Mrs. Wells again when her husband wasn't around. He had to walk around the builder's van on his way out.

He rang Miss Pratt's number but, when he got no answer, he tried Mr. Pegram instead. His wife answered and said that her husband should be back just before six. Mac said he'd call by a little earlier so he could interview her first.

The Pegram's house was just another council house on a big estate. It had three bedrooms and Mr. Pegram lived there with his wife, two young daughters and his mother-in-law. Before ringing the door bell, Mac had a look around the back.

An entryway ran along the back of the house and a six-foot wooden fence separated the Pegram's back garden from it. However even Mac wouldn't have needed a ladder. There was a concrete hydrant marker post that was around three feet high. Mac grabbed the top of the fence and stood on top of the post. There was a large plastic composter and an overturned plastic box right by the fence. It would have been easy to drop over the fence onto the top of the composter and then down onto the box.

Mac went around the front and rang the bell.

Mrs. Angie Pegram was in her mid-thirties and seemed to be dressed in some sort of pyjamas. She led him into the kitchen and lit up a cigarette from the gas ring of the cooker.

'It said in the report that you'd left the back door open. Is that right?' Mac asked.

She shrugged her shoulders.

'Yeah, we don't always remember to lock it, do we? I mean it's alright round here so why would we?'

'It also said that you only had an Easter egg stolen?'

'Yeah, really strange that. It's not as if we don't have anything worth nicking.'

'Do you mind if I have a look around?' Mac asked.

'Help yourself.'

The house was cluttered and a bit chaotic but it was clean enough. The one room that was pristine and freshly decorated was their daughters' bedroom. It was very pink and all the toys were tidied away and the bunk beds freshly made up.

Back downstairs he looked around the living room and he noticed a large tablet on the coffee table. It was new and of quite an expensive make.

'Do you always leave this here?' he asked.

'Yeah, Robbie uses it for the football mostly but it comes in handy when we want to take a photo. We keep all our photos on there too. It's much nicer looking at them on the telly rather than in an album.'

It was a strange burglar that would go past something so expensive and so portable to steal an Easter egg.

The sound of the front door opening announced the arrival of Mr. Pegram. He was in his late thirties, muscular but with a bit of a pot belly. His brown hair was nearly white with plaster dust. Mac showed him his warrant card.

'I'm surprised that you lot would want to come back again. It was only an egg, probably just those kids from down the road winding us up. Little sods they are.'

'What made you report it then?' Mac asked.

'I didn't, it was her mom that did that. She got all upset because she'd bought it especially for my daughter Beccy. She's a big Peppa Pig fan you see. Personally though, I wouldn't have bothered.'

'By the way where is your mother?' Mac asked Mrs. Pegram.

'She's picking up the kids from school and then she's taking them to my aunt for a couple of hours,' Mr. Pegram replied. 'They love going there, Auntie Ellen always makes a big fuss of them.'

Neither of the Pegrams could add anything else to the little Mac had already learned. He ran through the list of the names of the other victims again but all he received was blank looks.

Back in the car he dialled Miss Pratt's number and this time he got an answer. She said that she was going out in an hour so Mac drove straight to Radwell.

The house was a pre-war semi-detached and quite unusually for the area made of blue brick. A young cheerful looking brunette opened the door to him.

24

'Miss Alicia Pratt?' Mac asked while showing her his warrant card.

'Please call me Al. Come in.'

The first thing he noticed was the alarm box on the wall just down the hallway. It had been repaired.

The house was strange inside. The décor was modern, bright pastel colours, but the furniture was quite old, though all of it was in good repair. There were some unopened boxes stacked in a corner of the living room.

'Have you been here long?' Mac asked.

'No, I only moved in a few months ago. I've still got a lot of work to do on the house.'

She curled up on a beanbag while Mac sat on an old brown Chesterfield sofa.

'Is this about the Toblerone?' she asked with a grin on her face.

'It was a bit more than that though, wasn't it? The burglar forced a door open and then disabled your alarm. I notice that they've fixed it now.'

'Yes, the insurance company did that and then fitted a new back door the day afterwards.'

She looked so happy that he really didn't want to put ideas in her head but he had to ask.

'Doesn't it make you a little nervous knowing that someone's been in here while you were sleeping?'

She gave this some thought and then gave him a broad grin.

'I suppose it should but, if I'm honest, no. I've always felt safe in this house. Until last September I was living in student digs, five of us in a small house. I had people in and out of my room all the time whether I wanted them there or not.' She looked around her. 'This is all mine, all this space. I can shut the door behind me and keep the world out. It's bliss. Anyway, he only stole a Toblerone, he could have made off with a lot more if he'd wanted to. The flat screen TV's brand new and my laptop's worth quite a bit, it was right there on the table. Strange sort of burglar he must be.'

Mac couldn't have agreed more.

'What did you study?' Mac asked.

'History. I got a first and now I'm working in a bank,' she replied with a shrug and a wry smile.

'I take it that the house was left to you?'

'Yes, my gran died last year and she wanted me to have it. She knew how much I loved this house. As a kid my mom worked, so she used to leave me here a lot and my gran and granddad were great. They were lots of fun to be with.'

She stood up and gestured for Mac to follow her. On the mantelpiece over the fire there were a number of framed photos.

'Here,' she said handing him one. 'That's gran and granddad on their wedding day.'

The photo was black and white and showed a young couple in a formal pose. The man didn't look old enough to be in an army uniform. The girl was in a white dress with a veil and a small posy of flowers. She looked quite nervous. He could tell from the hairstyles and clothes that it must have been taken sometime in the forties.

'Did he fight in the Second World War then?' Mac asked somewhat puzzled at how old he'd be.

'No, he just missed it,' she replied. 'He was conscripted in 1947 when that photo was taken. He was only eighteen at the time. He did a couple of years abroad but thankfully no-one shot at him much during that time.'

She put the photo back on the mantelpiece.

'I like keeping their photo here. This is still their house as far as I'm concerned.'

'Do you mind if I have a quick look around?' Mac asked.

She didn't.

He had a look at the back door first. It was a new UPVC security door with multiple locking points and hinge bolts.

'What type of door was here before?' he asked.

'A wooden one, the same as all the others,' she replied.

Although the wooden doors were quite sturdy, they'd be far easier to force open that the one newly fitted. He counted the paces to the alarm box. It was only ten steps away but even so that meant that the thief would have had somewhat less than thirty seconds to disarm the alarm. He wondered if the thief might have already known where it was.

'Did you have any strangers call just before the break in?' he asked.

'No, not that I can think of, just friends and family.'

'Did anyone try to sell you something at the door or perhaps a repairman might have called? Has anything like that happened recently?'

She gave it some thought.

'Well, I did get some deliveries around that time but they were all for the garden so no-one came inside as far as I can remember.'

Once again, he ran through the list of names. He noticed that she reacted when he said Wells.

'Well, I used to know a Virginia Wells at school. We used to be friends, until I went to university that is. I'll have to remember to look her up on Facebook and see how she's doing.'

It felt like clutching at straws but Mac would check it out anyway.

He thanked her for her help and gave her his number. Again, he'd learned next to nothing except that it was once again confirmed that he was dealing with a professional.

He sat in the car and rang Mr. Wells who confirmed that there was no-one called Virginia in his family.

He looked at his watch. It was now nearly seven, somewhat later than he'd thought it would be. He rang his friend Tim who was already occupying table thirteen in the Magnets and told him he'd be there shortly. He only had Mrs. Foskett to go.

'You're here about the chocolate buttons?' she asked in wonder. 'Really I'd have thought the police would have had better things to do. Come in then.'

Mac followed the white-haired Mrs. Foskett inside. The house was an old labourer's cottage built in 1911 or so the plaque outside had informed him. The furniture inside looked nearly as old. It was all neat and tidy but the thing that immediately hit Mac was the smell of baking that was wafting in from the kitchen. It made his mouth water.

'Fairy cakes for the grandchildren,' she explained with a smile. 'They love my fairy cakes, especially when I let them ice them themselves.'

'Do you mind if I have a look?'

She followed him into the kitchen. It was very warm inside and he noticed that the window was slightly open. She noticed him looking at it.

'I'd been baking that afternoon too and that's probably why the window was left open. I must have forgotten to shut it properly.'

'And you're sure that they only took a bag of chocolate buttons?' Mac asked.

'Yes, that's all. I might not have noticed but the window was wide open when I came down in the morning. I checked and that was all that had gone. The memory's not always so good but I knew that I had them because I'd only bought them the afternoon before and I still had the receipt. I checked because I thought why would anyone break into a house just to steal a bag of chocolate buttons? Mind you, I haven't got much else worth stealing anyway to be honest, not on a widow's pension.'

'What made you report the burglary then?' Mac asked.

'Oh, I didn't. I told my daughter and she insisted on reporting it to the police. It was probably just some kid having a bit of fun, a waste of time in my opinion.'

He went back into the living room. It was a little cluttered especially with photo frames which covered the whole top of a large sideboard and just about every other flat surface in the room. He glanced at them, families at the seaside, men and women dressed to the nines for weddings, babies, kids in the back garden, birthdays, Christmas. Most were in colour but a few, including a man in uniform, were in black and white.

A family's history at a glance, Mac thought.

He ran through the list of names once more but all he got was a shrug of the shoulders and a shake of the head.

She was the last one he had to interview and he left her none the wiser. After all the questions he'd asked he didn't know much more than he had before he'd started. As he drove back to Letchworth, he couldn't help feeling more than a little frustrated.

Oh well, he thought, a few pints and a chat with Tim should cure that.

Chapter Four

Mac woke having slept through the night for the first time in ages. The deep tiredness he'd been feeling behind his eyes had gone. He looked at the clock, it had just gone eight. He smiled. He'd had just over nine hours of uninterrupted sleep. Being on a case was obviously doing him some good.

He sat up and then carefully stood up. He smiled again. The pain wasn't too bad and he thought that today might be a good day. Then he heard the banging from next door. He looked out as long scaffolding tubes were being dropped noisily on the ground by a large man in a hard hat.

The neighbours had warned him that they were having the builders in over the weekend to do their roof but he'd forgotten. He had planned to do some work at home but he decided to give up and drive into town. The upside of the situation was that he could now treat himself to a full English breakfast at the Magnets before he started work.

Tim was going to be away until the evening. He'd apparently been successful and sold quite a lot of furniture recently so he needed to replenish his stock. He was scouring some markets in Essex for bargain antiques so Mac decided to go to the quiet of his office for the day and examine the case files once again. He was also hoping that it might take his mind off his favourite football team. Aston Villa were playing in a local derby later in the day and going for a club record, the most losses in row.

He also hadn't checked his post for a while but he wasn't totally surprised to find that there wasn't any. Getting his detective business going was slower going than he could have possibly imagined.

As he waited for his laptop to fire up, he sipped at his coffee and thought. So, what do a plasterer, two retired people, a bank worker and a builder have in common? Their ages were all different and they'd apparently never heard of each other. They were spread over a three-mile area and there appeared to be no discernible pattern. Yet Mac knew that there must be a connection between the five properties but he was at a total loss to know what that might be. He buckled down and started re-reading the case files.

It was just after eleven when he noticed a shadow darken the pane of glass in the door. He had a visitor.

He heard a tentative knock on the door.

'Come in,' he said.

A young woman came in and seated herself.

She had chestnut brown hair and was dressed in a short jacket with a pastel blue blouse and a long skirt. The clothes were modern but still looked curiously old-fashioned in some way. Of course, he'd recognised her as soon as she walked in. She was the young woman he'd seen crying through the pub window just a few days before.

Mac could see that she was very nervous and uneasy.

'I wasn't sure that you'd be in, it being Saturday and all,' she said as she sat down.

'How can I help?' Mac asked, already intrigued.

'My name is Catherine, Mrs. Catherine Lynn.'

She offered her hand which Mac shook.

'I have a problem, an unusual one, I guess. I must admit that I didn't know who to turn to about it and then I saw your website. I wasn't aware that Letchworth had its very own detective.'

Mac couldn't help thinking that she wasn't alone in that.

She continued, 'Anyway, my father died recently, somewhat unexpectedly, and we need to access his safe. We're fairly certain that there's…something in there.'

31

The hesitation struck Mac.

'It would help if you could tell me who the 'we' is and what the 'something' might be,' he suggested.

She looked up to the ceiling and then stood up and took a few paces up and down before sitting down again.

'I take it that everything I say here will be treated in the strictest confidence?' she asked.

'Absolutely,' Mac replied.

'You promise that you'll never tell anyone outside of this room a word of what we're about to discuss?' she insisted.

'I promise.'

Mac wondered if she was going to make him swear on a bible but she seemed satisfied with his promise.

'Very well, the family solicitor and I suspect that my younger sister had been stealing from my father before he died,' she said giving Mac a sad look. 'Indeed, stealing quite substantial sums and other things as well. We know that there should be some evidence of this but we've looked everywhere and found nothing. I can only think that it must be in the safe. I'd like you to open it for me if you can. Can you?'

'I'm no safe cracker,' Mac said, 'but I've known a few in my time. I could try contacting one of them, I suppose.'

'I would be eternally grateful to you if you could.'

'Why didn't your father leave the code to open the safe?' Mac asked.

'He did but when we tried it didn't work,' she said. 'My younger sister also knew the code which is perhaps the reason why my father changed it.'

'So, you think that your father might have been aware of what your sister was up to?'

'Perhaps, for a short time at least,' she replied. 'He suffered from vascular dementia, Mr. Maguire. I must admit that towards the end he didn't know who or where he was most of the time but he did have some lucid days.'

'And you think that during one of these lucid days he placed some evidence of your sister's activities in the safe and then changed the code?' Mac asked.

'Yes, we think it's possible. My sister was away in New York the week before he died. He could have done it then.'

Mac gave this some thought.

'When did you find out about your sister?'

'The solicitor told me about his suspicions last Thursday. I must admit that it really upset me. I had absolutely no idea that anything like that had been going on.'

That was the day Mac had seen her through the pub window.

'I take it that the solicitor's office is near here?'

'Yes, it's on Station Road but how could you know that?' she asked.

'After you visited the solicitor's you sat outside a pub just up the road from here. I saw you.'

She looked surprised at this and more than a little embarrassed.

'Yes, I remember that I had to sit down for a minute, I was feeling a bit sick. It was the shock of hearing about my sister I suppose. I didn't think that anyone had noticed me though.'

'Tell me about your sister,' Mac asked.

'Well, Danielle's only a year younger than me but we couldn't be more different. I went to university, got my degree and then got married but she dropped out after only a few months. She went absolutely wild, drink, drugs and so on. I persuaded her to come home and after a while she seemed to be happy there. She looked after my father and for that I was very grateful. You see, he and I didn't always get on and anyway she'd always been his favourite. And that made it all the more unbelievable, you know, that she'd steal from him.'

'Did anyone else stand to gain from your father's will?'

'Only the housekeeper Mrs. Symonds as far as I know,' she replied. 'Everything else was to be split between Danielle and myself.'

'Then she was really stealing from you then, wasn't she?' Mac pointed out.

Mrs. Lynn looked surprised.

'Yes, I suppose you're right,' she eventually said.

Mac was thoughtful for a moment.

'Okay, if the solicitor confirms what you've said I'll see what I can do. I'll need his name and address and the address of your father's house. Will I need a key to get in?'

'Oh no, Mrs. Symonds still lives there. She'll let you in and look after you. Just tell her that I sent you.'

'I take it you'll want to be there if I do manage to open the safe?' Mac asked.

'No, I'm afraid that I can't. I'll be on holiday with my husband in Devon. Not a great time of the year I know but I desperately need to get away for a while and I love the walking there. That's how I met my husband you know, while I was hill walking...in Wales. We're both very keen walkers.'

Mac wasn't sure that this was information he particularly needed. He just nodded.

'Anyway, if you do manage to get the safe open please let me know straight away and I'll drive back and collect whatever you've found,' she said.

'Are you planning on pressing charges if there is anything incriminating in the safe?' he asked.

She shook her head emphatically.

'No, I couldn't do that to her. If anything has gone then the solicitor said he'll be able to adjust the settlement. So long as she agrees that is.'

'I'm sure she will, if the other option is going to jail,' Mac said.

34

Her face turned white.

'It wouldn't come to that, would it?'

'If the sums were large enough almost definitely, I'd say. Especially if the judge deems it to be elder abuse, they're quite hot on that these days.'

'Really?' she muttered.

Her face didn't regain any colour.

'Where's your sister now by the way?' Mac asked.

'As far as I know, she's gone back to New York.'

'What's her full name?'

'Danielle Pierson. My father was Thomas Pierson.'

Mac knew the name.

'That's Thomas Pierson, the painter?'

She nodded.

Thomas Pierson was something of a local celebrity. Over the last couple of decades, he'd gained a world-wide reputation and quite a few of his paintings were currently hanging in the National Gallery.

'Okay, if your solicitor confirms what you say then I'll see what I can do,' Mac said.

She gave him the solicitor's name and the name of his firm.

'Thank you very much, Mr. Maguire. Please call me on this number if you manage to get the safe open. I'll drive straight back and pick up the documents. Please don't tell anyone else about this and don't let Mrs. Symonds know about Danielle, in fact don't tell her any more than you need to. My sister may be, well a thief I suppose, but I don't want anyone else to know.'

'I understand.'

Mac had every intention of carrying on with his investigation into the Easter egg heists but he could put out a few feelers while he was doing this. He took out his mobile phone and flicked through his contacts. It was still there. Mac hoped that he hadn't changed his number in the last six months or so.

He hadn't.

35

'Now here's a blast from the past. How's it going Mac? I thought you'd retired?' a gruff Irish voice said.

'Hello Micky, how's business?'

Micky Milligan was heavily into recycling, recycling information that is. He'd tell anyone what he knew for a price. He was a walking encyclopaedia of crime which is why Mac had used him a lot when he'd been in the force.

'Oh, you know a pound here, a pound there. I get by. What do you need?'

'I need the name of a cracker. Do you know anyone?'

'Oh Mac, don't tell me that, after all these years fighting crime, that you've finally come over to the other side?'

Mac laughed out loud.

'No Micky, it's all totally legit. Someone's died and his family need the safe opening but they want to keep the police out of it. I just need someone who can open it without damaging whatever is inside.'

'Unfortunately, we're a bit short on talent in that department these days. Kids just don't have the patience for that type of work anymore. Well, if it's legit then why not ask Jimmy Carmichael? He's gone straight or so I've heard.'

'He's out of jail?'

'Yes, he got time off for good behaviour. I think he's living in your neck of the woods somewhere.'

Mac marvelled at the information that Micky kept in his head.

'Thanks Micky. How much do I owe you?'

'You can buy me a Guinness the next time you're in the area. Nice hearing from you again Mac. Take care.'

Mac made another call. If Jimmy was out then he'd be on probation. He knew someone in the service. He told them what he needed Jimmy for. They said they'd try and get a message to him.

36

Mac sat for a while thinking about Jimmy Carmichael. 'Robber Red' the gutter press had dubbed him while the Times had called him the 'Socialist Safecracker'. He was a very interesting man and Mac found that he was looking forward to meeting him again.

Having made his calls there was nothing else he could do, so he carried on reviewing the case files.

It had just gone one when he got a call from Andy. It looked like the thief had struck again except this time someone had been seriously injured. Mac arranged to meet Andy at the hospital straight away.

As he drove there, he couldn't throw off the feeling that it was all wrong somehow. Had the Chocolate Thief really gone over to the dark side?

Chapter Five

He drove to Stevenage and met Andy in the lobby of the hospital's Accident and Emergency department.

'Have you been to see her?' Mac asked.

Andy nodded.

'Unfortunately, she's asleep but the doctor says that she should be okay.'

'What do we know?' Mac asked.

'The victim is a seventy year old widow called Mrs. Doris Westwood who lives in Henlow. It looks as if she's fallen from the top of the stairs to the bottom. Nothing broken as far as they can see but she's had quite a bang on the head.'

'What makes you think that this is linked to the other burglaries?'

'The MO looks exactly the same, glass pane smashed at the back and the glass is gone,' Andy replied. 'She's likely to be asleep for a while. Do you fancy having a look around her house while we wait?'

Mac did.

He climbed into Andy's car. They drove to a white rendered terraced house on the High Street in Henlow. Andy opened the front door which led straight into the living room. It was a parlour with old-fashioned, but very well looked after, furniture and a couple of glass cases holding ornaments. Mac grew up in a house just like this and it felt incredibly familiar to him.

Just beyond the living room door there were some stairs on the right-hand side and beyond that a large kitchen.

'She was found here,' Andy said pointing to the foot of the stairs.

'Have you got the call?' Mac asked.

Andy took out his phone, selected the recording of the 999 call and passed it to Mac.

'999. What service do you require?' a woman's voice said.

Then another woman's voice but this time it was faint and weak.

'I fell... I fell...'

'Did you fall love? Are you hurt?'

'Yes, I fell....'

A moment's silence.

'We've traced your number. Are you Mrs. Doris Westwood living in Henlow?'

'Yes, Doris that's me...I fell.'

'Doris an ambulance is on the way. They'll be with you in a few minutes.'

'Ambulance is coming...'

'Doris are you still there?'

The line had gone dead.

'So, she managed to call in then,' Mac said. 'Where was she when the ambulance arrived?'

'Right there, where she fell,' Andy replied, pointing to the foot of the stairs.

The phone was on a sixties style telephone seat a good seven or eight feet away.

'No-one's moved anything have they?' Mac asked.

'Not as far as I know,' Andy replied.

'I take it that it was the landline she used if they could trace the call that quickly?'

'Yes, it must have been. She has a mobile phone but it was found upstairs on her bedside table.'

'Then how did she call it in?' Mac asked. 'I doubt she'd have got up and walked to the phone and then walked back and laid herself down again.'

'Yes, it looks like someone else must have been here,' Andy said.

Mac took the phone and walked towards the spot where Mrs. Westwood was found. The cable just about stretched.

'Let me hear that call again.'

Mac listened closely but, if there was someone else there, they were very careful not to let themselves be recorded.

They had a look around the house. It was full of the clutter of a lifetime but tidy enough. Mac looked at the ranked rows of framed photographs on a sideboard. The history of another family laid out before him; births, marriages, holidays and old black and white photos of men in strange suits and uniforms.

'Here look at this,' Andy said.

He showed Mac a supermarket receipt. It was time stamped just seven or eight hours before Mrs. Westwood had her fall. Mac read down the list and, near the bottom, there it was. A six pack of Mars bars.

'I take it that there's no Mars bars in the fridge or cupboards?' Mac asked.

Andy shook his head.

'So, unless she ate all the Mars bars in a few hours, it looks like it's definitely our man again.'

'By the way how did the paramedics get in?' Mac asked. 'I didn't notice any damage to the door.'

'Apparently it was open when they got here.'

Mac gave this some thought.

'Yes, it's the sixth burglary alright but this time it might have been a lucky one for Mrs. Westwood. I think it's quite possible that our man saved her life.'

What do you mean?' Andy asked.

'I think that when our man broke in, he found her lying at the foot of the stairs,' Mac said. 'He knew better than to move her just in case it might make her injuries worse so he brought the phone to her. She was just about conscious enough to say something and luckily it was enough to get the ambulance on its way. He even left the front door open for them. I wonder what he'd have done if she'd have been unconscious? Anyway, it could well be that Mrs. Westwood might have been lying there yet if he hadn't broken in. I still haven't been able to figure out what he was after though.'

'Yes, it's a puzzle, isn't it? But then again you like puzzles, don't you?' Andy said.

Mac smiled. Andy was spot on there.

Andy's phone rang.

'She's awake? Okay, we'll be right there.' Andy turned off the phone. 'Mrs. Westwood's woken up. Let's see what she's got to say, shall we?'

Mrs. Westwood had definitely been in the wars. Her face and arms were black and blue which clashed a bit with the wide smile she had on her face.

The doctor told them that they'd confirmed that nothing major had been damaged or broken just a lot of painful soft tissue injuries and a bump on the head. However, they were keeping her in for a few days just in case.

'Good afternoon, Mrs. Westwood,' Andy said as he showed her his warrant card. 'I'm DI Andy Reid. Are you okay to talk for a few minutes?'

'Oh yes, dear. I never turn down a bit of company.'

'How are you feeling?'

'A bit shaken I suppose but not too bad,' she replied with a smile. 'They're really looking after me in here, the nurses are very nice.'

'Can you tell us what happened?' Andy asked.

'Oh yes, I remember everything. I've already told the doctor. He was worried in case I'd lost my marbles but they're all still there, thank God. It was all Sparky's fault. God, she can be very stupid sometimes.'

'Who's Sparky?' Andy asked.

'Why, she's my cat of course.'

'So, how was it the cat's fault?'

'She usually sleeps on my bed but last night she wouldn't come into the bedroom for some reason,' she explained. 'So, I had to go out on the landing to get her. When I tried to pick her up, she ran between my legs and I nearly stepped on her. In trying to avoid hurting her I ended up hurting myself. I lost my balance and went head over heels down the stairs. I think I was unconscious for a while.'

'Do you remember making the phone call?' Andy asked.

'Yes, but it's all a bit hazy. I remember trying to move but I couldn't. I got really scared, I knew that I could be lying there for days.'

'Don't you have any family or people who visit you regularly?'

'My son lives in Scotland and he comes down as often as he can,' she replied. 'He's flying down here now, so the doctor said. He's asked me to go and live up there with him but I'd sooner stay where I am. I've got lots of lunch clubs and places I can go here but I like having my home to myself.'

'What happened next?' Andy prompted.

She screwed her face up.

'It's strange, like it was a dream or something. I felt a hand on my wrist which is what I think woke me up. I looked up at him, he was all black.'

'Are you saying that he was a black man?' Andy asked.

'He could have been dear for all I could see of him. No, I meant that he was dressed all in black, quite tight fitting it was too. He had a black balaclava on as well. God, I haven't seen one of those in years.'

'Was he a young man or an older man?'

'Oh, he was a young man dear, I could tell that from his figure. He had a nice bum too,' she said with a wicked little smile.

Andy and Mac couldn't help smiling too.

'Anyway, he brought the phone over and rang 999 and then held it so I could speak. Once the ambulance said it was on its way, he put the phone back then he stayed with me holding my hand until I saw the blue lights. I must have blacked out again because the next thing I knew I woke up here.'

'He never said anything at all?' Mac asked feeling as if he was clutching at straws.

'Not that I can remember, dear. Do you know who he is?' she asked.

'We think he might be a burglar, he's broken into some other properties too,' Andy replied.

'A burglar?' she said with some surprise. 'Well I say! I've never been robbed before so it must have been my lucky day when he broke in.'

'We think that he might have stolen a packet of Mars bars,' Mac said.

'He stole my Mars bars? Well, God bless him but he could have taken the whole house as far as I'm concerned.'

Outside the hospital Andy said, 'It's a strange case, isn't it? What type of burglar breaks into six properties, only steals chocolate and then saves a woman's life?'

'He might have been responsible for Mrs. Westwood's fall in a way,' Mac said.

'How come?'

'I'm wondering if the cat knew that there was someone strange in the house. Animals can be very good at that sort of thing and perhaps that why the cat's behaviour was different. Anyway, as you said, I like a puzzle and I'm going to keep at this one until I find the answer.'

'I'm really glad to hear you say that,' Andy said. 'It's starting to bug me a bit now too so, if you do find anything, please give me a ring straight away.' Andy looked at his watch. 'I'm going to knock off. I said that I'd give the wife a lift to the supermarket and I'm already late. I'll see you Monday perhaps.'

'Yes, I'll see you then,' Mac replied.

He went back to his office and the case files. Tim said that he should be back by six. Mac was glad because by the time six o'clock came he'd had enough. He'd not got an inch further and he decided that it was time for a drink.

He rang Tim who said that he was twenty minutes away. As he slowly walked up the hill towards the Three Magnets, he tried to let the facts swirl around his head and not to think too hard about them.

Six burglaries where only chocolate was stolen. All professionally carried out and all within a six-mile radius of Letchworth. The only problem was there was not even the hint of a clue as to why. Mac was certain that there was something that tied these six properties together. But what could it possibly be?

He opened the door of the pub and felt a sudden fear run through him. He sat down at table thirteen and, hands slightly trembling, he got his phone out. He was totally shocked and appalled by what he read. He went to the bar and got a round of beers with Irish whiskey chasers.

He knew that Tim would need a stiff drink when he heard the news.

Chapter Six

Sunday – Seven days before Easter

Mac woke up late having slept well once again. Even after having a wash he still felt a bit groggy and realised he might have had a pint or two more than normal the night before. He had good reason though.

He still couldn't quite believe it, winning 1-0 with two minutes to go and then the Villa let in a soft goal in the last minute. They then compound it by giving away a penalty in the last seconds of extra time. Even when the goalkeeper got a hand to the ball and it came back off the post, they still couldn't clear it and let the penalty taker side foot it into the corner of the goal on the rebound. After much discussion Tim and he had concluded that, if it wasn't for the players and the manager, then they might have a decent team. If it wasn't for the owner of course.

He'd almost begun to wish that his dad hadn't taken him to Villa Park when he'd been a child. Then he remembered the excitement of those Saturday after-noons nearly five decades ago. Holding his dad's hand tightly as he steered them safely through the swirling crowds converging on the football stadium. Bovril and corned beef sandwiches at half-time and the odd victory of course. He quickly withdrew his wish but still couldn't help feeling utterly frustrated when it came to his favourite football team.

As he made some coffee he thought about the case. This didn't make him any less frustrated though. Mac was at heart a great believer in there being some reason and logic behind everything, even if sometimes the logic might be more than a little warped. He just couldn't see any logic in this case yet, warped or not. Although it was Sunday, he wondered if there was something that he could do to push the case forward, even if only by an

45

inch or two. He suddenly remembered something, a question that they hadn't asked.

At the hospital Mrs. Westwood was more than happy to be interviewed again.

'I do love having a chat,' she said. 'I must say that the nurses and that are lovely here but they don't always have time for much of a chat, do they? Anyway, it's Sunday isn't it? I hope they're paying you overtime.'

Mac assured her that they did.

'I was just wondering if you'd remembered anything else since we last talked?'

She gave this some serious thought.

'Well, yes I think I did remember something but, as I said before, it all seems a bit like a dream now.'

'What did you remember?' Mac asked, hoping for even the shadow of a lead.

'I think he said something just before he touched my wrist.'

'Go on,' Mac said.

'Well, as I said I'm not sure but I think he said 'Hockey'.'

'Hockey? Are you sure? Just that word,' Mac said giving her a puzzled look.

'No, I'm not sure at all dear if I'm being honest,' she replied. 'Who knows, maybe I dreamed it.'

'How's your hearing?'

'Not bad, I had it tested not too long ago. They said I had the hearing of a forty year old,' she said giving him a bright smile.

Mac gave this some thought and then remembered the question that he'd come to ask.

'Do you know anyone with the surname Foskett, Llewellyn-fforbes, Pegram, Pratt or Wells?' he asked.

'Sorry dear, could you say them again but a bit slower this time?'

He did.

'Well, I do know a Wells, Colin Wells. He's my nephew. He was in not long ago with his wife and my son.'

'That's the Colin Wells who's a builder and who lives in Baldock?'

'Yes, that's him dear,' she replied. 'He's a lovely man. He's collecting Easter eggs you know, for the little children in hospital.'

At her insistence Mac stayed for a while as she told him all about Colin and the rest of her family. It took well over half an hour before a nurse came to take her blood pressure thus allowing Mac to gracefully slip away.

Mac sat in the car for a while and thought over what he'd learned. At last there was a real connection between at least two of the victims but Mac was doubtful as to its importance. In such a relatively small place if you picked six people at random it wouldn't be unlikely to find that some of them would know each other. It was the word that bothered him more.

Hockey.

What on earth did it mean?

He looked at his watch. It was now nearly one. Tim was off once again doing his rounds of the local markets. Mac would hear all about the bargains he'd bought tonight. What to do in the meantime though?

Although the connection was probably just a coincidence Mac thought he might as well follow it up. In the back of his mind he remembered that he also wanted to have a chat with Mrs. Wells without her husband being around. He had an idea that there was something she wouldn't say last time they'd spoken.

Mrs. Wells opened the door. She informed him that Mr. Wells was out.

'That's okay,' Mac said more than happy to find that she was alone. 'This will only take a minute.'

She invited him into the living room. The pile of Easter eggs had grown and took up at least half of the room. She saw Mac looking at the pile of confectionery.

'We normally worry that we won't have enough eggs to go around. Now we're worrying that we won't have enough children,' she said with a wry smile.

'Have you remembered anything since we last spoke?' Mac asked.

She shook her head.

'Are you sure that there's something that you haven't mentioned?' Mac said. 'Even if it's something that seems really trivial it could turn out to be important.'

She gave it some more though and shook her head again.

'No sorry, there's nothing.'

'Nothing?'

She shook her head with total certitude.

Mac felt somewhat deflated. He'd been so sure.

'Well, apart from one of my photos having been moved that is.'

Mac's heart almost skipped a beat. Could this be a real clue at last?

'Show me,' he said.

'Here on the sideboard,' she said pointing to a group of framed photos.

'And you're sure that one of them was moved by the burglar?'

'It must have been, I didn't move it and Colin knows better than to touch my pictures. I always have them in the same order see. First there's my grandad, that's him in his army uniform, then my mom and dad, then Colin's mom and dad and lastly our niece Mandy.'

'And what exactly was moved?' Mac asked.

'My grandad's picture was moved. It was more or less in the same place but it was at a bit of a different angle, if you know what I mean.'

'How can you be so sure?'

'Because it caught the light from the window when I looked at it from where I sit,' Mrs. Wells replied. 'I couldn't see the photo at all with the reflection from the window. I always have them positioned so I can see them from where I sit.'

She pointed to an armchair. Mac thanked her silently for being so pedantic.

'When the forensics people were here, did they fingerprint the photo frames?' Mac asked.

'I don't think so dear. I only found out that it had been moved after everyone had gone and I could finally sit down and relax.'

'Have you cleaned the frames since then?' Mac asked hoping against hope that she hadn't and that the thief might have gotten careless at last.

'Oh yes of course, I clean them every other day,' she replied. 'The dust gets on them otherwise.'

Mac inwardly sighed. He went over and picked up the photo frame. It showed a young man with black slicked back hair. He was in a World War Two army uniform and he had a lit cigarette in his hand. He was smiling brightly. For some reason Mac had the feeling that it had been taken before he'd gone off to war. Perhaps the smile was a little too bright.

'Can you tell me about your grandfather?' he asked sitting down again.

'Well, grandad Ronald was in the Army. He served abroad somewhere. I remember when I was kid hearing someone talking about their holidays in Spain and how nice it was going to a warm country. Grandad said they could keep their warm countries. He'd had more than enough of them during the war.'

'What regiment was he in?'

'I'm not sure if I'm honest,' she said shrugging her shoulders.

He remembered the photos of other men in uniform that he'd seen in some of the other victim's houses. He found that Mrs. Wells' grandfather interested him.

'Is there someone who'd know a bit more about your grandfather's time in the army?' he asked.

'You'd need to speak to my Aunty Pat. If anyone would know, she would. She's not far off eighty but she's still as sharp as a pin. She lives in a nursing home just down the road. I'll come with you if you like. I haven't seen her for a couple of days so a visit would be nice.'

She guided Mac and in less than a minute they pulled up outside the Convent Court retirement home.

Mrs. Wells waved at a woman manning the reception desk who pressed a buzzer to open the door. It was very warm inside and smelt of air freshener and urine. Mrs. Wells led them into a rickety lift that took its time to get to the floor above.

'She'll be in the lounge with the rest of them. She likes a good chat does Aunty Pat.'

She was right. Her aunt was one of a gaggle of elderly women seated in armchairs around a very large TV screen. She was a large woman who was also slightly deaf. Mac asked his questions and Mrs. Wells acted as interpreter, repeating each question loudly so that her aunt could hear.

'He's a polite man. Is that what you're saying dear?' Aunt Pat asked.

It took a few minutes for her to get the drift. Mac fed the first question to Mrs. Wells.

'Your dad, what regiment did he serve in during the war?'

'Now let me think,' Aunt Pat said. 'Oh yes, it was the Hertfordshire Regiment of course. He was in what they called the 'Letchworth Pals'. They were all from around here.'

'Where did he serve?' Mrs. Wells said even more loudly.

A number of the inmates were already giving her dirty looks.

'Oh, he was all over. He started in North Africa with Monty.'

'Where did he go after North Africa?' Mac asked.

She seemed to be hearing him okay now.

'Well, let's see. Yes, that's right more warm countries he said. He really didn't like warm countries. I remember him saying that the best thing that ever happened to him when he was in uniform was when he got back to England. He got caught in the rain as they left the plane and he said it was the most refreshing feeling he'd ever had in his life. He knew that he was back home then, you see, because of the rain.'

Mac looked at her and she eventually remembered that he'd asked a question.

'Oh sorry, silly me! So yes, after North Africa he went to Italy but he wasn't there long. Then he got whisked off to Greece along with all the other Letchworth Pals. They were there for nearly four years.'

Mac felt his heart speeding up.

'Greece? Why Greece?' he asked.

Aunty Pat screwed her face up with thought.

'Yes, I think it was because their Captain could speak Greek, well old time Greek I think it was. Anyway, granddad said that the Captain picked the language up in a few weeks and, while he got to learn a bit, he said that he never really got the hang of it like the Captain did.'

Another question occurred to Mac.

'He was there for four years? That means he must have been there until well after the war ended.'

'Oh yes, he was there until the middle of 1947 but God knows why. I remember asking once what he did in Greece but he wouldn't tell me. He said it was something he'd spent his life trying to forget or something along those lines.'

'What was your father's name?' Mac asked.

'Ronald Thompson. He was a sergeant when he came out. I saw his uniform once. Mom showed it to me and it had three stripes on the arms.'

For some reason Mac felt that he was on to something.

'So, your father really never said anything at all about his time in Greece?'

She thought for a while.

'Yes, strange that, isn't it?' Aunty Pat replied. 'He was there for years yet he never said anything about it to any of us. I think something happened there, something that made him a bit sad. I'm really sorry but I haven't a clue what it might have been.'

While he drove Mrs. Wells back home he asked her about Doris Westwood.

'Oh yes, poor Aunty Doris. We went to see her at the hospital this morning and she does look a sight. Still smiling though, God bless her.'

'We think that the person who broke into her house might be the same one who broke into yours.'

Her eyes widened in surprise.

'Really? Now there's a turn up for the books. He saved her life though the burglar, at least that's what Aunty Doris says.'

'Yes, it certainly looks like that,' Mac said. 'Is there any reason you can think of why the burglar might have picked you and your aunt?'

'I've no idea. We're not exactly millionaires either of us, are we? Anyway, I'm glad that he broke into Aunty Doris's, she's one of my favourite relatives.'

Mac thought about what he'd been told as he drove back. Almost without thinking he found himself outside of Monty Llewellyn-fforbe's house.

His granddaughter opened the door. She had blonde full-length hair, an oval-shaped face and a naturally pale complexion. Mac thought that she was very pretty. He introduced himself.

'Oh, you're the detective!' she said excitedly, her face breaking into a wide grin. 'I've never met a detective before. I'm Helena. Come in and I'll take you to Monty. He's in the billiard room.'

From the size of the house Mac wasn't surprised that it had a billiard room. He'd been to smaller leisure centres. However, Monty wasn't playing when Mac and Helena entered the room. The whole surface of the table was covered in photos.

Monty cleared his throat before saying, 'Mr. Maguire, I hope you've come to tell me that you've got the culprit and that he's safely behind bars.'

'I'm sorry but no. I've not found anything definite as yet.'

'Nothing definite?' the old man said with some exasperation. 'Your three days are up today and, as I'm paying, I'd like to know exactly what you've found so far.'

Mac had forgotten all about the three days.

'You don't have to worry about paying me as I've been working with the police on this case,' Mac said. 'There have been more break-ins reported in the area, break-ins that are very similar to yours. As I'm investigating them all it wouldn't be fair to charge you.'

Monty had a photograph in one hand and a pen in the other. Mac noticed some photographs face down in a pile. They all had something written on the back.

'More break-ins you say?' the old man said his anger clearly rising. 'What's in God's name has happened to Letchworth? I can remember when someone getting prosecuted for being a litter-bug would make the front page of the local papers and now it's break-ins here, there and bloody everywhere.'

As he spoke Monty's face got red and Mac feared for the old man's blood pressure.

'As with you though, nothing was stolen. Apart from the chocolate that is,' Mac pointed out.

'It's still a bloody cheek though. So, who do you think it was then? Was it some of those young layabouts with nothing to do that I see hanging around the Job Centre in town?'

Mac noticed Helena looking up to the ceiling as he said this. She obviously didn't agree with his sentiments.

'No, it definitely wasn't one of them,' Mac replied. 'Whoever carried out the burglaries was a professional.'

The old man stopped and placed the photograph and pen on the billiard table.

'For God's sake what would a professional thief be doing stealing chocolate?'

'That's what we'd like to know,' Mac replied. 'Personally, I think that it was just a blind. I think that he might have been after information of some sort.'

'Information? I thought everything in the world was out there on the bloody internet or whatever they call it.'

'Not quite everything. Do you know anyone who was in the Hertfordshire Regiment during the war? The Second World War that is.'

'Of course, my father was a Captain in the regiment during the war,' Monty replied.

Monty scrabbled around amongst the photographs. He passed one to Mac.

It was a small square black and white photo and showed a man in his thirties in uniform. He was wearing shorts, long black socks, a short-sleeved shirt and a peaked cap. He was squinting into the sun. In the background Mac could see a small church. It was white-washed and had a tiled roof and a round tower with a cross on the top. It was obviously somewhere abroad, somewhere Mediterranean, Mac guessed. He turned over the photo. In faded ink it said 'Agiou Athiris 1946'.

The man in the photo wasn't smiling and, even in such a small photo, Mac could see that there was something about the man's eyes. They had seen things. He looked very like Monty.

'He was an Ancient Greek scholar, wasn't he?' Mac asked.

He could see the look of surprise on Monty's face.

'Yes, he was a professor but how the devil could you know that?'

'I spoke to the granddaughter of one of the 'Letchworth Pals'. Her grandfather was Sergeant Ronald Thompson.'

Monty stood still for a few seconds while he thought.

'Yes, yes', he said, a memory dawning on his face. 'I remember. After the war, it might have been the early fifties I suppose, I was about fifteen or so and I remember my father talking about a Sergeant Ronnie Thompson. He'd met up with him and they'd gone for a drink or something. He didn't say what they'd talked about, just that he was a 'good man in a scrap'. Yes, those were his exact words. It was just about the only thing he ever said to me about his time in Greece.'

'He was there quite a while I believe,' Mac said.

'Yes, I think that he was there for some years. He never mentioned the war much but, on the rare occasions that he did, it was always about North Africa or Italy but never Greece for some reason.'

'Apparently, Ronald Thompson never said much about his time in Greece either. That's quite strange, isn't it?' Mac asked.

'Yes, I suppose it is. I've often wondered what happened there.'

Mac wondered if the same thought had occurred to Monty. Bad things happen in wars. It might have been seventy years ago but Mac couldn't help wondering if the past was somehow coming back to haunt the Letchworth Pals.

Chapter Seven

Monday – six days before Easter
Mac woke up early and he was eager to get up and get on with things. At last he had a lead.

His back pain was still there but thankfully it was no worse than normal. He felt quite rested as he'd had a quiet night in. Tim had been off again at some antiques market near Bath and hadn't got home until late so Mac had just stayed in and watched some television. By luck there was a series about the history of Ancient Greece on and Mac found it quite fascinating.

His lead might be tenuous as he'd only connected two of the break-ins so far but he still felt that he was on to something. However, he was careful in not allowing himself to get too carried away with the thought. He knew that he had a lot more digging to do before he could start constructing any theories about the case.

At Monty's suggestion Mac's next call was at the Regimental Museum in Hertford. He'd looked it up on the internet. It was only open on alternate days but luckily one of those was today.

The Museum, in fact three rooms in an annex at the back of County Hall, was crammed with glass cases and odds and ends. Dominating one wall behind the small reception desk was a large flag. It was a Union Jack but it had a shield in the middle with some Roman numerals on it. It was stained and there were holes in it.

'They're bullet holes. Believe it or not but that flag survived the Battle of Brandywine Creek,' a voice behind him said.

Mac turned to see a tall grey-haired man coming towards him. He was slightly stooped and he was wearing an old tweed suit and waistcoat. He guessed that the man wouldn't be far off Monty's age and, like Monty, he seemed sprightly enough.

'Brandywine Creek?' Mac asked.

If it was a battle then it was one that he hadn't heard of before.

'Yes, the Forty-Ninth Regiment of Foot as it was known then. It was one we actually won. We lost the war though.'

Seeing Mac's look of incomprehension, he continued, 'The American War of Independence 1777. I'm Terence Hurdlow, how can I help?'

'I was wondering if you had any information on the regiment and where it fought during the Second World War?' Mac asked.

'Oh yes, we've got loads on that. Any particular time and place?'

'Yes, Greece, around 1943 to 1947, I think.'

Terence's eyebrows raised.

'Really? Strictly speaking the regiment wasn't involved in Greece, except for a small unit that is.'

'Do you have any information on that unit?' Mac asked.

'Yes, we do actually. Just the one document, a journal as it happens.'

He disappeared into a small room behind the desk and returned with a small battered notebook.

'This is the journal of Private Edward Chappell. It was donated to the museum by his family after he died. He was too young for the war but he was conscripted shortly after it ended.'

Just like Alicia Pratt's grandfather, Mac thought.

'It covers the period 1946 to 1948 if that's any help,' Terence asked.

'It might. Is there any chance I could borrow it?'

Terence looked aghast at the prospect of the journal leaving the premises.

'Oh, I'm sorry but we couldn't do that.'

Mac showed him his warrant card.

'Of course, we'll do everything to help the police but I couldn't let this out of the museum. It's a unique record. However, we do have a digital copy if that would help?'

'Yes, a copy would be fine.'

A thought struck Mac.

'Tell me, do you keep a copy of all the documents here?'

The old man shook his head.

'Oh no, that would be far too expensive. We only make copies upon request and I'm afraid that we normally have to charge for them.'

'So, I take it that someone else has previously requested a copy of this journal?' Mac asked.

'Yes, just a few months ago I think it was,' Terence replied.

Mac was very interested to know who that might be.

'Do you remember who it was?'

'Not the name, I've never been great at names, but it was a young chap. He looked foreign to me but he spoke perfect English. Very polite he was, nice chap.'

'I take it that you keep some sort of record of such transactions?' Mac asked crossing his fingers.

'Of course, I'll be just a moment.'

Terence disappeared and came back with a large notebook. He opened it and showed an entry to Mac. It was dated some seven weeks before. The rest of the entry read –

'Digital PDF copy of catalogue item HR2341 –Journal of Pte. Chappell – Received £45.'

Next to this entry there was a signature but Mac couldn't quite make it out. He looked at the previous pages. There were only around thirty entries per year. He flicked back through the pages. No-one had requested a copy of the journal in the last twenty years or more. He turned the notebook back to the latest page.

'Is it okay if I take a photo of the page?' Mac asked.

'Yes, I suppose so. Do you have a camera with you then?'

Mac pulled out his phone and took a photo of the page.

'Dear me, I always forget that those things have a camera,' Terence said. 'I used to think that it was amazing enough when you could only speak through them.'

'And the copy of the journal?' Mac prompted.

'Oh yes, I'll have to get Stella to send it to you. I'll need your email address if that's okay?'

'Who's Stella?' Mac asked.

'She works at County Hall and helps us out with all the technical bits like the scanning of documents. I honestly wouldn't have a clue how to do it,' Terence said with a shrug.

Mac wrote down his email address.

'Did you send a copy out via email to this man?' Mac asked pointing at the signature on the copy.

Terence thought for a while.

'No, we didn't. He gave me one of those little rectangular things and asked if Stella could put it on that.'

'A memory stick?'

'Yes, that's it,' Terence confirmed. 'He came back a couple of days later and picked it up.'

No luck there then.

'Have you read the journal yourself?' Mac asked.

'Oh no,' Terence said, shaking his head. 'If I read all the documents that we keep here then I'd never have time for anything else.'

'I hope you don't mind me asking but were you in the regiment too?' Mac asked.

'Oh yes and my father before me.'

'So, your father was in the Second World War?' Mac asked.

'Yes of course, mostly North Africa.'

'Did he ever mention a Captain Llewellyn-fforbes?'

60

Terence screwed his face up with concentration.

'That name sounds familiar alright. Was he a professor by any chance?'

'Yes, Ancient Greek.'

'I vaguely remember something my father said once. He said that this professor was a decent chap but he came to a sticky end. In fact, most of his unit did.'

'How?' Mac asked eager for the answer.

'I'm sorry, I did ask my father but he wouldn't say anything else. All I know is that they were all sent home in some sort of disgrace. He seemed upset about it though. He said that it had stained the reputation of the regiment or something to that effect.'

'Is there any chance that there might be a record somewhere of what happened?' Mac asked hopefully.

'I doubt it. According to my father it was all very hush-hush. There wasn't a court-marshal or anything like that, they were all just very quietly discharged.'

Even if it hadn't come to court, it still sounded as though something very serious had happened in Greece. For some reason Mac felt that this was important and that it might have a direct bearing on the case.

'Thanks. Could you ask Stella to get that copy to me as soon as possible?' Mac asked.

Terence assured him he would.

Mac sat in the car for some time looking at the signature on his phone. He blew it up on the screen as much as he could. He smiled broadly when he finally worked it out. Even with the magnification it had taken him five minutes but he was now fairly sure that the signature was that of a 'Mikis Theodrakis'.

His smile faded as he realised that he'd heard that name somewhere before. He looked it up on the internet. He knew from the number of results that it wasn't good news. Mikis Theodrakis was indeed one of Greece's most renowned composers and musicians. He wrote the music for the film 'Zorba the Greek'. Mac remembered seeing it on the television when he was young. He'd forgotten most of the story but he remembered the music well enough.

It's not all bad news though, Mac thought. Leaving a Greek false name would imply that the person who left it was Greek too. But why? Why was a young man so interested in events that had happened some seventy years before?

He had a really bad feeling about the whole thing. Monty's father had never spoken about what had happened to him in Greece and now Mac had found out that he and most of his unit were considered as a disgrace to their regiment. He desperately wanted to know why and he hoped that the journal might hold the clue.

Chapter Eight

Mac gave some thought to his next steps while driving back towards Letchworth. He was in Stevenage when his phone rang. He pulled over and took the call.

'Is that DCS Maguire?' a man's voice asked.

It was a voice Mac hadn't heard for a few years but he knew instantly who it was.

'How are you, Jimmy?'

'I'm okay. I got a message that you wanted to see me. I'm not in any sort of trouble, am I?'

'No, it's nothing like that. Are you free now?' Mac asked.

'No, I'm at work at the moment. I finish around six if you want to meet up around then.'

'Where are you?'

'I live in Welwyn now,' Jimmy replied. 'Can you tell me what this is all about?'

'I've got a job for you. I'll explain later if you don't mind,' Mac said.

They agreed to meet at a local Welwyn pub, The Doctor's Tonic.

Speaking to Jimmy reminded him that he had another call to make. He decided he might as well get it out of the way now.

Meghart and Johnson Solicitors were on Station Road and they had a spacious set of offices above an estate agency. He asked the young receptionist for Kevin Acourt. She went away and came back. She told him that Mr. Acourt would be free in ten minutes. Mac glanced around the office while he waited. It was prosperous looking and very busy. He had to pull his legs in several times as very serious looking people in very dark clothes strode by him carrying armfuls of legal documents. Finally, one of them stopped and introduced himself.

Kevin Acourt was in his mid-thirties, well-dressed in a sharp charcoal grey suit, crisp white shirt and blue tie.

He was younger than Mac had been expecting. Most solicitors he'd met in the course of his duties seemed to have been born fifty.

'Mrs. Lynn said you'd be visiting. It looks like a bad business,' he said shaking his head.

For some reason Mac felt that there was something a little false about the solicitor but, then again, most solicitors he'd met seemed to put up some sort of front. However, he decided that he was going to observe Mr. Acourt closely.

'How did you find out about Danielle?' Mac asked.

'It was more by luck than anything else really. When Mr. Pierson was diagnosed with dementia he signed two forms giving Lasting Power of Attorney. His daughter Danielle assumed responsibility for his health and welfare while my firm was given the responsibility of looking after his property and financial affairs.'

'Why wasn't Mrs. Lynn involved?'

'I believe that she and her father didn't get on all that well, so she was quite happy with the care arrangements as they stood. Danielle had always been Mr. Pierson's favourite so she thought that he'd be happier being looked after by her anyway.'

'So, what did you find that made you suspicious of Danielle?' Mac asked.

'I'm afraid that Mrs. Lynn hasn't authorised me to say,' the solicitor hastily replied. 'All I can really tell you is that she's anxious to get her hands on those documents so that she can sort this mess out with her sister as soon as possible.'

Mr. Acourt then gave him an insincere smile. Mac decided to throw a rock in the pool and see if it made any ripples.

'You don't suppose that the reason Danielle was in America was to sell some of his paintings, do you? I hear they're very sought after over there.'

The smile left the solicitor's face and his face whitened. Mac felt that he'd scored a direct hit.

'I'm afraid that I can't comment but please don't take this as confirmation of anything you've just implied.'

His composure and the insincere smile were back.

However, Mac now knew that when Catherine Lynn spoke about 'substantial sums' she really meant it. He'd looked it up. The last Pierson sold at auction went for over three hundred and fifty thousand dollars.

He left the solicitor to it.

As he left the office, he looked at his watch. It was just before one o'clock. Mac checked his emails. One of them was from a Stella McTavish and it had an attachment. Mac decided to go home and start on the journal. He stopped on the way and bought a new print cartridge and a pack of paper. If he had to read for any length of time, he found that he took it in much better from a printed copy than from a computer screen. He set up his laptop, downloaded the attachment and started printing the journal off.

While the printer chugged away, he made himself a sandwich and watched the birds feeding in the back garden. Once everything was printed off and in order, he laid the stack of printed paper on the dining room table. He looked at the first page –

'The journal of Edward Chappell, Private of the Hertfordshire Regiment. In the event of death please return to Mr. Samuel Chappell of Gt. Wymondley, Herts.'

Another local lad then. Mac looked him up on the internet. He found an obituary on him from one of the better local papers. Apparently, Edward had started as a reporter and eventually became editor of the paper. He'd held the post for many years before retiring.

So, he became a journalist, Mac thought. The journal should make for good reading then.

He set the alarm for five o'clock in case he got too pre-occupied. He didn't want to miss his appointment with Jimmy Carmichael.

Edward's handwriting was luckily quite legible. Mac remembered being taught it when he was in primary school and sighed. Even he couldn't read his handwriting these days.

He quickly skipped through the early part of the journal. This covered his training and the trip to Greece. This seemed to take quite a while as the ship stopped off at Gibraltar and Italy on the way. He disembarked in Greece at Piraeus and spent most of a very hot day in the back of a truck before he and two other men were left in the town square of Agiou Athiris. They hadn't had the temerity to ask what they should do when they got there so they just stood in the square looking at each other until a loud voice ordered them to attention.

They followed a sergeant down a dusty road for a half a mile or so until they came to a long low white-washed building. A hand painted sign outside told them this was 'The Broadway Gardens Barracks, Hertfordshire Regiment.' Edward looked around at the rocky scrubby land surrounding the barracks and found himself already missing the greenery of home.

The sergeant took them to meet the Captain who Edward described as 'tall and thin and having an air of natural authority'. Edward then did Mac a big favour. He listed all the men's names in the unit. He had obviously done this so he could learn their names by memory.

'The Old Guard

Captain Harry Llewellyn-fforbes – top brass of the unit. Strange name, even stranger spelling!

Sergeant Thompson – His bite is even worse than his bark, better do as he says or else

Corporal Pegram – doesn't seem as much of a stickler as the sergeant thank God

66

Pte. Andy Shoreham – doesn't say much

Pte. Johnny Foskett – bit of a comedian, nice chap

Pte. Ted Daniels – doesn't say much either but seems alright

Pte. Benny O'Shea – could talk the hind leg off a donkey

Pte. Barney Posnett – cook – not bad either, even if he tries his hand at some of the local grub at times

New Guard

Pte. Tommy Saunders – Career soldier, kit is always spot on. The others have already started calling him 'Blanco'

Pte. Alfie Pratt – Another conscript, my age, a good lad and we're becoming friends already

And Me'

Mac was quite surprised when the alarm went off. He thought about what he'd read so far as he drove to Welwyn. All the names except one were on that list but there was no Westwood. However, that might be because, like Mrs. Wells, Westwood was her married name. He'd have to ask her what her maiden name was.

Mac spotted Jimmy sitting in the corner of the pub. He sat unmoving with his hands on his lap, a glass of sparkling water in front of him. Jimmy was the stillest person Mac had ever come across and, therefore, one of the hardest to read. Mac got himself the same and joined him.

Jimmy stood up and offered Mac his hand.

'It's been a while,' Mac said as he shook it firmly.

'It has,' Jimmy confirmed as he sat down again.

'How long have you been out?'

'Seven months,' Jimmy replied.

'How long did you do in the end?'

'Only eighteen months. I was in an open prison for most of it.'

'How was it?' Mac asked.

'It was okay actually. They taught me gardening there and I loved doing that. I won some awards too, you know at local gardening shows and that. I've tried but I haven't been able to get a job working outside yet, not even in a garden centre. It's my record,' Jimmy explained. 'I won't lie about it, although I must admit that I've been tempted to.'

'So, what are you doing now?'

'I'm working in a warehouse. It's okay but it's all indoors. I really enjoyed working out of doors when I was doing the gardens. Anyway, it looks like that will be coming to an end shortly anyway. There's going to be some redundancies, so it's last in, first out.'

'So, I reckon you could do with some money then?' Mac asked.

'I certainly could. I'm married now and there's a baby on the way.'

Mac gave it some thought. He was going to offer him three hundred to do the job but he changed his mind.

'I've got a job for you, a safe. Five hundred and it's totally above board.'

If he had to, Mac reckoned that he could make up the extra two hundred himself.

'I'd expect no less from you but five hundred is a bit more than I was expecting,' Jimmy said. 'How many safes do you want me to crack?'

'Just the one. When are you free?'

'I could have a look on Friday afternoon, around three. My shift finishes at two.'

'That will be fine,' Mac replied. 'The job's only in St. Ippolyt's. I'll pick you up here if that's okay.'

It was. Jimmy didn't stay for any chit-chat.

Mac sat there for a while and then decided to go to the hospital and see Doris Westwood again.

She was more than happy to see him. Mac thought that she was looking much better now that the bruising had started to fade away a little.

'Hello love. Have you got more questions or are you just feeling a little lonely tonight?' she asked with a twinkle in her eye.

'A bit of both probably. When I was in your house, I saw an old photo of a man in uniform. Was that your father?'

'It could have been my dad or my husband, I've got photos of them both on the sideboard.'

'I take it that they were in the army?' Mac asked.

'Oh no, nothing like that, they were both RAF men, aircraft mechanics,' she explained. 'My dad, Herbert Swithenbank, came down from Yorkshire during the war to assemble Hurricanes, that's why he was based at Henlow. He was there for the whole war so he was. Then after the war he taught my Derek aircraft maintenance and that's how we met.'

She then gave him a potted history of her family and was just getting started on her second oldest nephew when the nurse came to give her some medication. Mac took the chance and slipped quietly away.

As Mac drove back to Letchworth, he thought about what he'd learned. The last burglary seemed to contradict his theory that the break-ins were linked to men who had served in the Hertfordshire Regiment but Mac was beginning to think that it might just prove the opposite. He needed to talk to Tim.

He drove home and rang Eileen. The downside of her being a one-woman taxi company was that she wasn't always available. Mac was always a bit disappointed when he rang and got the recorded message telling him that she was off-duty. He'd gotten to know her over time and it had become more like getting a lift from a friend than anything else. Luckily, she was working and Mac had a nice chat with her on the way to the pub.

Fifteen minutes later he was sitting at table thirteen in the Magnets opposite his friend Tim. They had a little more than half a pint left but, when Tim heard that they were about to discuss a case, he got up and went straight to the bar to get another round in.

'Just so we don't have to interrupt ourselves,' he explained when he returned.

Mac took him through what he found in some detail. Mac could tell that Tim wasn't totally convinced with Mac's lead.

'I mean it's all just based on a photo frame having been moved,' Tim pointed out. 'Might it just be a coincidence that they all had relatives in the same army unit? I mean Letchworth is a fairly small place.'

This was why he liked talking things over with Tim. When he'd been in the force, he had his sergeant Peter Harper. He was always willing to shoot one of his pet theories down in flames if he saw a flaw and, of course, he had always had his Nora.

'Well you might be right,' Mac conceded, 'but I can't help thinking that there's something to it.'

'What about the last one though? What was her name again?' Tim asked.

'Doris Westwood.'

'Well, her father was in the RAF and, even if he had have been in the army, it wouldn't have been the Hertfordshire Regiment,' Tim stated.

'Why's that?'

'Because Henlow's in Bedfordshire.'

'God you're right, so it is,' Mac said. 'It being so close I forget that Henlow's in another county. Anyway, it might still fit my theory. This is what I think's been going on. Something happened seventy years ago in Greece and, after all these years, someone's interested in finding out more about it. I think that this someone got hold of the journal and found out the names of the men in the unit. They were then able to trace their relatives...'

Mac suddenly stopped in mid-sentence. Tim had seen him like this before and didn't attempt to interrupt his friend's thoughts.

'Sorry,' Mac apologised. 'Where was I? Oh yes, they traced their relatives and then broke into each house looking for something. As nothing was stolen, apart from chocolate, I can only think they were after information of some sort. I think they found what they were looking for at Monty Llewellyn-fforbes house.'

'What makes you think that?' Tim asked.

'Whoever's behind this is quite clever. The last burglary was a total red herring as it was not only an RAF family but also someone from outside the county. I think that they're trying to make the pattern a bit harder to spot. Also, if Monty's had been the last burglary, we might have concluded that they found what they were looking for and would want to look a bit closer at that one.'

'That sounds plausible,' Tim said. 'By the way why did you stop just now?'

'It suddenly hit me where my next stop should be, the County Records Office. I think that must have been the chocolate thief's next call after finding the journal.'

Tim gave this some thought.

'So, they first of all find the journal and get a list of all the men in the unit who were in Greece. Then they work out who their relatives were and then systematically break into each relative's house until they found what they were looking for. So, in that case there shouldn't be any more break-ins, should there?'

'I'd bet on it,' Mac replied.

'Have you any idea yet what they might have been looking for?'

'Not a sausage,' Mac said as he shook his head.

Thinking of sausages made him realise that he was hungry.

'I'll need to read more of the journal. I'm hoping that it might shed some light on the whole thing but we'll see. Anyway, that's not the only case I have on at the moment.

I'm also going to be doing a bit of safe cracking,' Mac said with a smile.

'Safe cracking? I hope you've not finally gone rogue in your old age?' Tim asked teasingly.

'No, it's all above board. An old man died and didn't leave the code to his safe. His daughter has asked me if I could find someone to open it for them.'

'Oh, that's okay then. And have you found someone?'

'Yes, one of the best I ever came across too,' Mac replied. 'I met him earlier this evening. It's the first time we've seen each other in a few years.'

'I take it that you were professionally involved as it were?' Tim asked.

'Yes, but not in the way you mean. He helped me solve a case of attempted murder a few years back.'

Mac told Tim the full story.

'It sounds as if you quite liked him,' Tim observed.

'Yes, I did. He was a thief sure enough but he never stole for himself and all the people he took money from could well afford it. The papers called him 'Robber Red' or the 'Socialist Safe Cracker' but mostly 'The Taxman'.'

'Yes, I think I remember something about him now. One of the papers reckoned that most of the money he made from the robberies ended up being given to charities.'

'Yes, mostly homeless charities too. It came out in the trial that his family had been homeless more than once so you can understand that. Anyway, he has his own rules and as far as I know he's always stuck to them. In all his robberies there was never any violence involved, apart from the last one I suppose.'

'Tell me,' Tim said.

'Well, he'd planned to rob an extremely wealthy Arab prince who was in London for the casinos. Somehow Jimmy had found out that this prince had a safe stuffed full of bank notes, mostly pounds and euros, and Jimmy's aim was to relieve him of it. He'd planned it meticulously and had made sure the prince was in the casino before he started cracking the safe. Judging by his previous visits, he knew the prince would be in there for hours. However, it was just pure bad luck that the prince had to go back to his office, something to do with a sudden drop in the price of oil, and he caught Jimmy at it.'

'So, what did Jimmy do?'

'Nothing,' Mac replied. 'The prince had two minders with him and they kicked him around the room for a while before they bothered to call the police. Jimmy didn't even try to defend himself.'

'What happened then?' Tim asked.

'He got two years for breaking and entering, even though it was a first offence.'

'That doesn't sound like much considering he was The Taxman,' Tim commented.

'I reckon that the judge gave him a bit less than he might of because of the battering he'd taken. Anyway, they couldn't prove he was the Taxman as there wasn't anything to connect him to the other burglaries. If they had, he'd have gotten a lot more than two years, but they never found the note.'

'The note?'

'Yes, the Taxman always left a note saying 'You have been taxed',' Mac said. 'They thought that he might have just had time to shred it, so they took the contents of the shredder and tried to piece them together. They found nothing.'

'So, what's he doing now?' Tim asked.

'Working in a warehouse in Welwyn Garden City. From what he said I think he hates it though. He was in an open prison and they taught him gardening. He won some awards too, or so he said. Knowing Jimmy, I'd bet his gardens were good. He never does anything by halves.'

Mac had a thought.

'You meet a lot of people who have big gardens, don't you? If you ever hear that someone's after a gardener let me know.'

'The record would be a problem though,' Tim said with a frown.

Mac could only agree. He decided that a break in the proceedings was required.

'A pint and a foot-long hot dog?' he asked.

Tim didn't say no.

Chapter Nine

Tuesday – five days before Easter
Mac had looked up the opening hours before he went to
bed. The Records Office at Hertford opened at nine. He'd
set his alarm for seven.

He slept well and was once again grateful that his
back was no worse than normal. He was on a good run
for once. He decided to read a few more pages of the
journal while he ate breakfast.

*'Been here three days now and it's not what I was
expecting. The old guard aren't all that keen on carrying
out their duties and seem to do as little as they can get
away with. They all seem down in the dumps. I asked
Benny about this and all he said was that 'We're now
helping the people who were our enemies to catch the
people who are our friends.' This was followed by quite a
few choice swear words. He wouldn't say any more about
it which, for someone who would normally gab about
anything, I thought was very strange.*

*It was also strange that it was Ted Daniels, one of the
quiet ones, who finally explained the situation to me and
Alfie. He said that, when they got sent over in forty three,
they were fighting alongside a partisan group 'up there'.
He pointed to the high mountains that more or less
encircled the town. He said –*

*'They were good men and a good laugh too once you
got to know the lingo a bit. We fought side by side,
summer and winter. We lived in caves and stole sheep
and any other food we could get our hands on to survive.
There were good friends, both British and Partisans, who
never made it down. They're buried together up there. So,
between us we helped push the Germans out of Greece
and what thanks did they get? When the Yanks and our
top brass took over, they put the bastards who we'd been
fighting back into power. The local army colonel here
was a Nazi collaborator and most of the police were too.*

75

They were the cowards who kowtowed to the Germans while the real men were up in the mountains fighting.'

I asked him why things had turned out that way.

Ted said that -

'The top brass are afraid that the country might go the same way as Albania and Yugoslavia and become a communist country. So what if they want to do that I say, it's their country anyway, isn't it? I mean God knows I'm no Red myself but some of the Partisans we fought with were communists and they were some of the best blokes I've ever met. I'm bloody sick of it, none of us has any idea what we're still doing here. They say that we know the territory and that they want us to chase our pals around the mountains. Meanwhile, we have to smile at the Nazis with their fancy uniforms whose throats we'd have happily cut not so long ago. The scum strut around the place like they own it. Problem is they bloody do now.'

Ted stopped and walked off. I could see that he was getting very upset. Me and Alfie talked about it and we both came to the conclusion that we wished to God we'd been posted somewhere else.'

Mac reluctantly put the journal down. It was time to go.

The Records Office was at County Hall, not far from the Regimental Museum he'd visited the day before. A young lady dressed in jeans and a top that didn't quite cover her midriff explained that he'd have to make an appointment. He showed her his warrant card. She changed her mind.

'Do you get many people coming in here doing family research?' Mac asked.

'Not as many as you might think. We get the odd person now and then researching their own family but its professional researchers who visit us the most. We have a couple who are in and out of here all the time. Oh, and sometimes the doctors of course.'

'Doctors?' Mac asked.

'Yes, we sometimes get doctors from the University researching how a patient's family members had died and so on,' she explained. 'We also get a few epidemiologists from time to time who do more historical research.'

'Do you keep track of what people look at during their research?' Mac asked hopefully.

The girl smiled and shook her head.

'No, I'm afraid not. Once they've applied and been granted access then we just let them loose on the database. It's quite safe as they can't change anything, they can only look.'

'So, you don't keep any records of who comes in and out?' Mac asked.

'I didn't say that. We like to know who's looking at our records and we have to get them to sign in and out anyway for fire safety reasons.'

She showed him the visitor's book. After signing it himself Mac took it to a nearby table and looked closely at the entries. A couple of names were repeated again and again. The professional researchers Mac guessed. He turned the pages back to around the date that Mr. Theodrakis had signed for a copy of the journal. There were only three possible candidates – James Allsopp, Margaret Turnbull and Dr. John Snow. That last one started a tickle in Mac's brain. He got his phone out and looked the name up on the internet.

He got a myriad of results about some character in a TV show that Mac had heard of but never watched. Tucked in amongst them were a few entries for '*John Snow (1813-1858), a British physician considered one of the founders of epidemiology...*'

Mac read the entry and remembered that he'd read about this doctor before. Dr. John Snow was the first person to prove that the killer disease cholera was spread through contaminated water and not through the air. Mac wondered if this was another false name and how many people might know about John Snow who weren't a doctor.

He took the book back to the receptionist.

'I'm sorry but what's your name?' Mac asked.

'Tracy, Tracy Harrison,' she replied.

'Tracy, do you always check what people sign in as?' Mac asked.

Tracy gave it some thought.

'No, I don't suppose we do. We just check their identity or pass or whatever they've got. But why would someone sign in with another name?' she asked.

'What about this one?' he asked pointing to Dr. John Snow's signature.

'Sorry, no,' she replied after giving it some thought.

No luck there then. He asked about the other two signatures for James Allsopp and Margaret Turnbull but had no luck there either. He took photos of the signatures.

He then asked Tracy if she could get him any information about any possible descendants of Ted Daniels, Benny O'Shea, Barney Posnett, Tommy Saunders and Andy Shoreham.

She smiled widely. Mac thought that she was very pretty when she smiled.

'Thanks, it'll be nice to have some proper work to do for a change. Give me an hour or so and I'll see what I can come up with,' she replied.

Mac decided to sit in the car while he thought of what his next step should be. Dr. John Snow, he knew that it was probably a false name but even false names can tell you something. They can tell you that someone is Greek and perhaps that they're also a doctor. He compared the Theodrakis and Snow signatures. They looked very alike but, then again, he was no handwriting expert. He knew the lead was tenuous in the extreme but Mac decided he was going to follow it up anyway.

78

An hour and ten minutes later Tracy gave him her results.

'Unfortunately, I've found nothing on Benny O'Shea, I presumed his first name was Benjamin, or on a Thomas Saunders who would be around the right age. That might simply be because they moved out of the area after they came back from the war. However, I did find out something about Andrew Shoreham and Edward Daniels. Andrew Shoreham got married in 1950 but had no children. He died in 1989 and his wife died two years afterwards. As for Edward Daniels, I'm afraid he died in 1952. He never got married or had any children as far as I can tell.'

'What was the cause of death?' Mac asked.

Tracy consulted her notes.

'Suicide I'm afraid. The causes of death were formally given as 'Dysthymia', which we'd know better as depression nowadays, and gas poisoning. He probably stuck his head into an unlit oven, it was quite a popular way of killing yourself back then. However, its better news when it comes to Barnaby Posnett. Here unusual names really help. He married in 1950 and had a son, Robert Posnett, five years later. Robert should still be alive as I haven't found a death certificate for him.'

'Perhaps he moved as well?' Mac suggested.

'Oh no, he still lives in Letchworth, well up until last year anyway. I looked him up in the Electoral Register.'

'So, you have his address too? That's brilliant,' Mac said with a smile.

She wrote down the address. Apparently, Mr. Posnett lived two streets away from Mac.

Once he was back in the car, Mac looked up the University Medical School on his phone. It was situated at the campus in Hatfield. He decided to go there first, as he wasn't too far away, and he'd interview Mr. Posnett later.

It took him less time to drive there than it did to find the Medical School once he was there. The campus was huge and the school was right in the centre of it, somewhere. He got sent from building to building until finally a receptionist admitted that he was actually in the right place. He showed her his warrant card.

'I'm looking for any information on a doctor who I believe might work here. Can you help?'

The woman smiled broadly at him and said, 'No.'

She explained that he'd need to go to the University's HR office. She must have seen the look of frustration on Mac's face so she gave him a map of the campus and carefully drew the route that he should take. Even so he got lost again.

Eventually, in yet another building, yet another receptionist said, 'Yes, please take a seat and I'll give the person you need to speak to a call.'

Mac gave a sigh of relief. Ten minutes later he was met by a smartly dressed middle aged woman who asked him to follow her. Luckily her office wasn't too far away and no stairs were involved. Once they were seated Mac showed her his warrant card.

'I'm Mrs. Cresswell. How can I help the police?' she said with a bright smile.

'I'd like you to check whether or not you have any Greek nationals on your staff.'

'Please be aware that due to the Data Protection Act I can only give you some basic information. I'd need a formal request from the police before I could hand over any personal details.'

'I can arrange that but, in the meantime, I'd be grateful if you to confirm whether or not you have any Greek nationals on your staff and, if you do, where they're from.'

'I think I can do that,' she replied.

She consulted her computer and a remarkably short time later said, 'Yes we have two, a Dr. Christodoulou and a Dr. Soulis.'

'And can you tell me where exactly in Greece they come from?' Mac asked.

She looked at the computer again.

'Yes, Dr. Christodoulou is from Athens and Dr. Soulis is from Kalamata.'

The last name sounded familiar.

'Kalamata? Do you know where that is?'

'Southern Greece, it's where the olives come from.'

Of course! Mac mentally kicked himself, he'd only been looking at a can of them the other week in the supermarket.

'I'll need their current addresses and any other information you can give me on them.'

'I can do that but only once I have the official request,' Mrs. Cresswell insisted.

He'd just have to wait then.

Before he left, he had Mrs. Cresswell write down her email address. Once in the car he rang Andy and asked him to send the data request as soon as he could. Andy said he would and suggested that they meet the next morning for a catch up.

Mac drove back to Letchworth letting the new facts he'd learned rattle around his head. He pulled up outside the address he'd been given. Luckily Mr. Posnett was in.

Mr. Posnett, now sixty-one, lived only with his wife, his two children having left home. He worked at the District Council Offices in the Housing Department.

'Have you noticed anything unusual in the past week or so?' Mac asked.

Mr. Posnett and his wife looked at each other and shrugged.

'I don't think so...' Mr. Posnett replied a little unsurely.

'Oh, there was the chocolate!' his wife said, interrupting her husband.

'He doesn't want to know about the chocolate...'

This time it was Mac who interrupted.

'Tell me about the chocolate,' Mac said.

'Well, Robert here still thinks I ate it, I'm sure, but we had one of those big bars of chocolate in the fridge and when I came down the next morning it was gone!' she said in wonder.

'Were there any signs of forced entry, broken glass, anything like that?'

'Oh no,' Mr. Posnett replied. 'I checked everything and all the windows and doors were locked.'

He gave his wife a look which indicated that he still thought that she was responsible for the chocolate being missing.

Mac had a look around. The back door was held shut by an old latch lock. There were bolts fitted to the top and bottom of the wooden door.

'Do you usually bolt the door at night?' Mac asked.

From the looks they gave each other it was clear that they didn't.

Mac looked in the recesses of his wallet band and found an old plastic card. It was a membership card for the police gym club and it must have been lurking in there for years.

Mac went outside and pulled the door shut. He inserted the card into the space between the strike plate and the latch. It took him less than ten seconds to open the door.

They both looked at him with open mouths.

'I think that you should get yourselves a new lock. When was the chocolate stolen?' Mac asked.

Mr. Posnett gave him the date. It was the same night that the Wells' house had been broken into. There was a good chance that this just might have been the very first break-in.

'Were we really broken into?' Mr. Posnett asked in some wonder.

'It looks like it,' Mac replied.

Mrs. Posnett gave her husband a very 'I told you so' look.

'But why? We're not rich or anything,' he said.

'I know it might sound crazy,' Mac said, 'but the only link I've found so far is that most of the others had a father or grandfather serving in Greece during the Second World War. I believe that your father served there too.'

'Yes, yes he did. He was in Greece for quite a while, not that he ever told me much about it,' Mr. Posnett said. 'He was a good cook though and he sometimes used to cook Greek food for us all when the weather got warm. I must admit that I really got a taste for it.'

'He never said anything at all about his time in the army, especially when he was in Greece? Please think hard, even something trivial might turn out to be important.'

Mr. Posnett thought hard as instructed.

'Sorry, he never said a word but I did find something after he died. He kept it in his sock drawer, would you believe.'

Mr. Posnett went over to the mantelpiece and came back with a framed photograph. It showed three men grinning widely. They were peeling potatoes.

'That's Dad in the middle but I don't know who the other two are.'

Mac knew. One was Alfie Pratt and the other was Edward Chappell. Alfie looked just like the photo taken on his marriage day and Edward hadn't changed all that much as he gotten older. He asked if he could look at the back of the photo. He carefully took it out of the frame and turned the photo over.

'Two new recruits working for their supper' was written in faded ink.

He turned it over and looked again at the men's faces. From the smiles Mac guessed that this photo was taken before the event that would change all their lives.

He took a photo of the photo, thanked Mr. and Mrs. Posnett and left.

It had been a long day but he found that he couldn't wait to get back to the journal. He made a pot of coffee and started on the stack of printed paper. He was feeling quite excited as he desperately wanted to find out exactly what had happened in Greece all those years ago.

There was quite a bit about the heat and the mood of the rest of the unit and even more about being bored and a lot of description about some of the chores that Edward had to do, including endless potato peeling. All in all, they seemed to spend half their time unsuccessfully chasing the Partisans around the mountains and the other half hanging around the barracks.

'The men are all bored stiff. The Captain no longer allows them into town as there was trouble the last time they went in. I didn't go but I was told that the Sergeant and the Corporal took on six of the local police and won. The Captain paid the bar owner for the damages out of his own funds.

This posting is like being in limbo. All the men just seem to be waiting to go home. They don't want to be here and they definitely don't want to catch any Partisans so it's all a bit pointless. I just wish something would happen.'

About ten pages later it seemed that Edward had gotten his wish.

'Just in case something happens I just want to let you know that I've ripped the preceding pages out myself and burnt them just in case. I also now hide this journal as I don't want it to get into the wrong hands, especially after the events of last night.

Since then our barracks have been crawling with military police and we've all been questioned several times. Alfie, Blanco and myself have followed the Captain's advice. In questioning we simply said that we noticed nothing unusual and that we all slept well last night as usual. We also said that we weren't close to the rest of the unit and that they've never told us anything of their feelings about being here.

Luckily, they seemed to believe us and so the New Guard at least appears to be off the hook. The Captain and the Sergeant, however, have been questioned non-stop ever since the balloon went up. First it was the Military Police and then a General arrived in a big fancy car. I knew it must be really serious if the top brass were getting involved. I heard the General shouting at the Captain, he called him a traitor and accused him of 'going native'. I heard that the Captain stayed silent and never said a single word throughout the whole investigation as did the sergeant and the corporal too when they asked him.

After the hullabaloo was over every one of the Old Guard were told that they were going home. Not dishonourably discharged, as they couldn't actually prove anything, but the nearest thing to it. They were told that they'd never get any of the medals they've earned. None of them seemed to mind this very much though, in fact they threw a party. It was clear that they just wanted to get back home as soon as possible.

Unfortunately for them, and especially the Captain, there was a real sting in the tail. The day before they were due to leave the Greek Colonel, a slimy toad if ever there was one, invited the unit to the town square. We were joined there by the town dignitaries and quite a crowd of the locals too. The Colonel had his men drag the priest out of the church and then they kicked him around the square right in front of us.

The Captain translated for us. The Colonel said that the priest was a collaborator and that he would be punished for it. This wasn't exactly news. The priest was a local man and even I knew that he favoured the Partisans, everyone did. The Captain then told the Colonel that accusing someone of being a collaborator was rich coming from him, someone who'd happily licked the Nazi's boots for years.

The Colonel looked like he was about to explode. I noticed that he kept looking right at the Captain as the beating took place. I felt that the whole show was really just for him.

The Colonel ordered his men into the church to look for evidence. They ransacked the place. We could hear the noise of things breaking from the square. Shortly after some smoke could be seen coming from one of the side windows. The police all ran out of the church.

In ransacking the place some idiot had knocked over some lit candles.

The Captain shouted something in Greek. I was told that he was screaming at the crowd to get water to stop the fire.

The Colonel had his men point their guns at the crowd. He walked up to the Captain and spoke to him in English.

'No water,' he said. 'Let it burn.'

He smiled straight at the Captain as behind him orange flames started to come out of the front doors.

So, we just had to stand there and watch the church burn down. I'd had a look inside once. It was cool and dark and had the smell of holiness. The thing I remember most though was the icon. They called it 'Our Lady of Agiou Athiris' and it had been in the church for centuries. I was told that every Easter they had a procession around the town and the icon was the centrepiece. I can only say that it was more beautiful than anything else I'd ever seen. Now it would burn along with everything else in the church.

The Captain strode off. I could almost see the steam coming out of his ears. I felt like crying myself. The colonel smiled at his back and, at that moment, I would *so have loved to have given him a bunch of fives right in the teeth. I saw the Captain drive off in the jeep a few minutes later. The crowd shouted and cried and some tried to break through the line of soldiers but, in the end, all we could do was stand and watch the white-washed church walls turn black with smoke. We all just stood and watched as the roof eventually fell in leaving just the blackened walls standing.*

All of the Old Guard were quiet that night. The truck came for them in the morning and that was that. Alfie, Blanco and me had the barracks to ourselves for over two weeks before replacements arrived. The new Captain is different. Like me and Alfie he's never fought in a proper war. He's all gung-ho about fighting the Partisans though, communist scum he calls them.

I can only say that I can't wait to get back home. In my heart I find that, like the old Captain, I have no taste at all for what we're being asked to do.'

Mac scanned the following pages but there was nothing relevant to the case to be found. He felt frustrated as though he'd gotten to the end of a murder mystery and then discovered that someone had torn out the last page.

He knew that something had happened in Agiou Athiris, something important enough to warrant a big investigation and to get most of a unit sent home. But what was it? He couldn't help thinking of My Lai and similar atrocities that had been covered up during wartime. He hoped to God that something like that wasn't involved.

Mac now wanted to find the mysterious Mr. Theodrakis and Dr. John Snow even more desperately.

He wanted that last page.

Chapter Ten

Wednesday – Four days before Easter
Mac had a restless night. The pain was bad and, turn and toss as he might, he couldn't find any sort of position that would give him the slightest ease. It was just before five o'clock when he gave up trying and got out of bed.

He gingerly stood up and then groaned out loud. The pain in his lower back was quite a bit worse than normal. He took his morning pills and decided he needed to be doing something to take his mind off it.

He read through the journal again while he sipped at a coffee. He was hoping that he'd missed a vital detail somewhere but unfortunately nothing new jumped out at him. He wondered about the soldiers in the unit and what it must have been like for them. To have fought for two years alongside men who had become close friends only to be then told that they were now the enemy and the enemy were now friends. It all sounded like something from Alice Through the Looking Glass.

He was meeting Andy at nine and he wondered what he could do in the meantime. His thoughts were interrupted by his phone ringing.

It was Andy. Mac looked at the clock. It wasn't even seven yet.

'I'm glad you're up. I know it's early but I'm on my way to Robert Pegram's house. He was one of the people who were broken into, wasn't he?'

'Yes, he was. What's happened?' Mac asked.

'He was stabbed late last night in his back garden by someone dressed in black, so he said. I only got the message a few minutes ago and I thought you might be interested.'

Mac was. He told Andy that he'd meet him at the Pegram's house.

They arrived at the same time. A uniformed policeman guarding the house let them in. Mac noticed that some uniforms were already doing some door to doors further down the street.

The house was empty, forensics had obviously completed their work. Andy led Mac through the front door, into the kitchen and then into the back garden. He noticed that Mac was limping but said nothing.

'Before they put him under Mr. Pegram stated that he got up in the night for a drink of water and saw some movement in the back garden. He went out to investigate. He saw what he first thought was a shadow but it turned out to be a figure dressed from head to toe in black. When he confronted him, the intruder pulled a knife and stabbed him three times. The scuffle woke up his wife. She called the hospital at two fifteen and the ambulance arrived three minutes later.'

'Three minutes?' Mac said in surprise.

'Yes, the ambulance station is only just over the other side of the main road,' Andy replied.

Mac remembered. He must have passed the station a hundred times or more but he'd never actually seen an ambulance coming out of it.

'It sounds like our burglar, doesn't it?' Andy asked.

Mac gave this some thought.

'If I'm honest I'd be a bit disappointed if it was. One night he saves an old woman's life and then the next night he's stabbing someone. That doesn't make much sense to me. There was a description of the man who broke into Doris Westwood's house in the local paper last night, wasn't there? They called him the 'Dark Angel' or something along those lines.'

'What are you getting at?' Andy asked.

'I'm not sure yet. How is he?'

'They were prepping him for an operation the last I heard. That's why I thought that we might come here first and have a quick look at the crime scene.'

Mac pointed to the fence.

'I had a look the last time I was here and it's easy enough to get over that fence from the other side. It's made even easier by the composter and that box being where they are. Did his wife see anything?'

'Apparently not but I'd like to confirm that for myself,' Andy replied. 'Come on let's go to the hospital and see what Mrs. Pegram has got to say.'

At the hospital a doctor told them that Mr. Pegram had lost a lot of blood and that the operation was still in progress. He said that he would live though and that he was a very lucky man. The knife blade had just missed vital organs twice, the third injury being more superficial. He told them that it would be a while before they would be able to speak to him.

Angie Pegram was in the relative's room being comforted by an older woman. Her mother Mac presumed. She looked dazed.

'What happened?' Andy asked her.

She gripped her mother's hand tightly. She didn't look at either of them while she talked.

'I'm not sure. I heard noises and I went downstairs. The back door was open and I could see Robbie lying in the garden. I ran out to him. He was covered in blood. I rang for an ambulance and luckily they were there in no time.'

She looked up at them both.

'Did he say anything?' Andy asked.

'Yes, a man in black did it. That's what he said.'

'What were his exact words?' Mac asked.

She thought for a while.

'He said, Angie, a man in black stabbed me. Tell the police. That's what he said. He said it twice.'

'Did you see anything yourself?' Andy asked.

She shook her head.

'Okay, I hope your husband will be better soon. We'll be back later.'

She didn't seem to be too excited about that prospect.

Outside the hospital Andy asked, 'So what do you think?'

'I'm not sure but I can't shake the feeling that there's something here that just doesn't quite add up.'

'What makes you think that?'

Mac shrugged.

'I wish I knew.'

Andy looked at his watch.

'It's only just past nine. There's not a lot else we can do until Mr. Pegram gains consciousness and we get the forensics report. Anyway, I need to get back to work on this exercise we've got coming up.'

'I bet that you'll be glad when it's all over,' Mac said with some sympathy.

'You can say that again. Okay, give me a ring if you get any ideas.'

'I will and can you email me a copy of the forensics report as soon as it comes through?'

'Sure thing,' Andy replied.

Mac sat in the car for a while letting it all run through his head. A little tickle at the back of his brain was telling him to look again. This tickle was very like an itch and Mac decided that he was going allow himself the luxury of scratching it.

The constable guarding the Pegram's house allowed him entry once more. He wasn't really sure what he was doing there but he knew that there must be something. He looked in every room of the house trying to get a picture of the family. Thinking of pictures, he sat down on the sofa in the living room and picked up the tablet from the coffee table. He found the pictures file, it had four hundred and nineteen items in it. It didn't take as long as he might have thought to scroll through them.

He stopped at a particular photo. It was in black and white and showed three men in World War Two army uniforms. They were on board a ship of some sort. They all had cigarettes in their hands and were smiling at the camera. The text said 'Grandad Pegram and some friends'.

Mac could see it in his mind. The burglar inserting a memory stick into the tablet and simply downloading the entire file of photographs. It would only take a minute or two. He placed the tablet back on the table.

He went into the kitchen and looked out of the window. He could still see blood on the grass. He looked over at the fence that the knife wielder must have come over. The composter and the plastic box next to it caught his attention again. He looked at them for a long time allowing the little tickle to grow and blossom into an idea. He smiled.

So, that was how it was then.

He now had a theory but he needed some proof. He went back to the tablet and started scrolling through the photos again. He was only interested in any that were taken in the back garden. He found a photo of the two daughters who were on two pink bikes with stabilisers. It was date stamped as last Christmas Day. The composter was in the same position but there was no box there.

He scrolled on and found another photo of the two daughters in the garden. This time they were with their grandmother. The box was now there right next to the composter. The time stamp was January 28th. So, the box had been there for nearly two months. It definitely wasn't the burglar then who had arranged an easy way of getting over the fence. Mac had a strong feeling that it might be all Mr. Pegram's doing. He also had an idea why.

He went to the front door and spoke to the constable.

'I saw your lot doing some door to doors earlier. Have they finished yet?'

'Yes sir, I think so sir,' the young constable said a little uncertainly. 'They started before seven and they've done most of the street, I think. A lot of people weren't too happy about it, us waking them up that is.'

'Do you know if anyone was especially upset at the news of Robert Pegram's stabbing?' Mac asked.

'I'm not sure but I can check.'

Mac waited while the constable phoned in.

'According to the sergeant, a Mrs. Tomelty just up the road started crying when she was told. He had to come back half an hour later to interview her, when she'd calmed down a bit.'

'What did she say?'

'Nothing of any use apparently,' the young constable said.

'Why was she so upset then, did she say?' Mac asked.

'According to the sergeant she said that she knew the family a bit.'

Mac would bet that she knew one member of the family very well. Mac got the house number. He was going to pay Mrs. Tomelty a visit.

Luckily, she was still in.

She was in her thirties, not bad looking, hair dyed blonde and obviously took quite a large cup size in her bras. She looked exactly as Mac had envisaged her.

Her eyes were red and she clutched a tissue in one hand.

Mac showed her his warrant card.

'I've already spoken to the police,' she said tersely, trying to shut the door.

Mac's foot stopped it closing.

'And you'll talk to them again,' he said. 'Shall we do this inside or do you want all the neighbours to hear what I've got to say?'

She reluctantly held the door open for him. She denied everything at first and he had to winkle it out of her. Eventually though, he and Mrs. Tomelty had a full and frank discussion.

While he walked back to the Pegram's house he got the number of the forensics team. Luckily the team leader was still on shift.

'The Pegram case, I'm just interested in knowing what areas of the house you processed. Did you do inside the house at all?'

'No, we were told that all the action took place in the garden so we processed that and both sides of the fence.'

'So, you didn't do the kitchen for example?' Mac asked.

'No and we didn't the living room or bedrooms or the house next door either. We only have so much time you know,' the team leader protested.

Mac thought that he sounded tired, so he thanked him and ended the discussion.

He stood looking at the house for a minute or two while he thought. He made a decision.

He ordered the young constable to follow him inside.

'We're going to search the house from top to bottom and we'll do it together so, if we do find anything, then there'll be a witness. Is that okay?'

'But I'm supposed to be guarding the front door...'

Mac gave him a stern look.

'Okay,' the constable said, 'but it would help if I knew what we were looking for.'

Mac told him.

'Where do we start?' the constable asked.

'As we're in the living room we'll start here then the kitchen and then upstairs.'

Forty minutes later they'd searched every room and found nothing. He went down to the kitchen to get a glass of water. The young constable followed him.

'So, what do we do now?'

'We search again. It has to be here somewhere,' Mac said with certainty.

He wished that he was as sure as he sounded.

After he'd washed the glass, he turned to say something to the constable when a flash of pink caught his eye. He stood looking at it for a few seconds as a smile formed on his face.

'Here, give me a hand,' Mac asked.

He opened the washing machine. It was full, mostly of clothes belonging to the two daughters. He soon found what he was looking for. He didn't see it at first as a pair of girl's leggings, pink of course, were tightly wrapped around it. Mac then showed it to the constable but he didn't make any attempt to retrieve it.

He phoned Andy.

'I'm sorry to interrupt but there's something you're going to have to see. Bring someone from forensics with you.'

Chapter Eleven

Andy and Mac both stood and watched as the forensics technician carefully removed the item from the washing machine without disturbing the leggings encasing it.

'I'll have to unwrap it in the lab,' the technician explained. 'If the leggings wrapped themselves around it early on in the wash then they might contain some trace evidence.' He looked at the control panel. 'It was on a forty degree wash so we might be in luck.'

Andy took a photo of it on his phone before the technician took it away.

'Come on,' Andy said. 'Let's go to the hospital and see what Mrs. Pegram has to say about this.'

At the hospital they were told that Mr. Pegram was still unconscious. The operation had been a success and he was 'making progress' or so the doctor told them. Mrs. Pegram was by his side holding his hand.

'I'm sorry but can we have a word in private?' Andy asked.

She just nodded and followed them. Mac thought that she looked worried.

Once in the relative's room Andy said nothing. He just showed Angie Pegram the photo. It showed the leggings and the clear outline of a long-bladed kitchen knife.

She turned white and sat down heavily, almost as though her legs had given way.

'What happened?' Andy asked.

He allowed her a minute or so to gain her composure.

'It was that bloody bitch Yvonne down the road. She used to be a friend of mine but, after her husband ditched her, she was all over my Robbie. He's such a fool, he's goes weak at the knees if any woman lets him know that she fancies him, especially ones with big tits.'

'I take it that he was visiting Yvonne Tomelty late at night?' Andy asked.

'Yes, and I was so stupid that I didn't cotton on for quite a while. Then one of my so-called friends started taking the piss and let the cat out of the bag. Just about everyone knew it seems, except for me of course. Anyway, it all made sense then. We've always liked a bit of a drink at night but lately I've been getting quite legless and falling asleep on the settee. That's because he'd been making my Bacardi and cokes a lot stronger and, once I'd nodded off, he was over the fence and down the road to that blonde bitch. You can guess what him and that slag were up to.'

'I take it that you went easy on the drink last night?' Mac asked.

She nodded slowly.

'I pretended to be a bit drunk but I'm afraid my pot plant got most of my drinks last night. Poor thing's probably dead by now.'

'So, what happened?' Andy asked.

'I waited and waited until just after two o'clock when I heard him getting back over the fence. I'd gotten so angry sitting there in the dark thinking about it and every minute that went only wound me up even more. By the time I heard him getting back over the fence I think that I'd honestly gone a bit mad. I took the knife out of the drawer, ran into the garden and stabbed him. I can't explain it. I know that people say that they saw red when they did something terrible but I really did. At the end, when he was lying on the grass and I saw the blood dripping from the knife, it was like I'd just woken up from a bad dream only to find that it was all real. I rang for an ambulance and Rob kept saying 'tell them a man dressed in black did this, just tell them that'. While the ambulance men were putting Rob on a stretcher, I popped the knife in the washing machine and then turned it on before I left the house.'

She shook her head as though to she was trying clear it.

'I still can't believe it happened. It's like I'm inside a nightmare and I can't wake up.'

They were interrupted by a doctor who told Mrs. Pegram her husband was conscious and that she could see him for a moment.

Andy showed the doctor his warrant card.

'Is it okay if we have a word too?' Andy asked.

'So long as you make it fairly quick. He'll probably be asleep again in a few minutes.'

Mr. Pegram had drips and tubes attached, his chest was strapped up and he looked in a sorry state.

He held his wife's hand tightly.

'Rob, these men are from the police,' she said. 'I've told them everything.'

He glanced at Andy and Mac and tried to smile.

'I don't know what she's told you but she's upset, so don't take any notice.'

Angie started crying.

'It's no good love, I've told them now. It was all my fault, I'm so sorry,' she exclaimed in between the sobs.

'No, it wasn't, it was mine. I thought you didn't love me any more so I gambled with my family, with you and the girls. I was stupid Angie but I'm not gambling anymore.' He turned his head to look at Andy and Mac. 'There was a man dressed all in black and he stabbed me. Angie came down a few minutes later and found me. Then she phoned the ambulance. Isn't that right Angie?'

All heads turned to look at Angie.

'Isn't it, love?' Rob asked again, his eyes entreating her to give the right answer.

Angie dabbed at her face with a tissue.

'It's no good love, they've found the knife.'

Tears started running down Robert Pegram's face.

'It's all my fault. I shouldn't have done it. I love you Angie.'

'I love you too Robbie.'

She turned to Andy.

'I know I have to go but can I stay with him until he falls asleep?' Angie asked.

'Yes stay. I'll send someone to pick you up in a while,' Andy said.

As he walked out Andy rang for two uniforms to pick up Angie at the hospital in half an hour.

'What do you think will happen to her?' Mac asked as they walked out.

Andy shrugged.

'She's got kids and, if her husband sticks by her, I'd bet she might get off with a Community Order. If she gets the right judge that is.'

'I hope she does somehow. After all they do really love each other.'

'It's a shame that she had to stab him to find that out though,' Andy said as he looked at his watch.

It had now gone twelve.

'I've had no breakfast!' Andy exclaimed.

'And mine was a long time ago. However, I know a place that does a nice all-day brunch,' Mac replied.

Comfortably seated in the Magnets in front of a large plate of egg, sausage and chips Andy asked him how the Easter egg case was going. For some reason Mac didn't want to say too much right at that moment, especially about the connection with Greece. Although he was fairly sure he was on the right track, he still didn't have anything concrete as yet.

'I'm not sure if I'm honest,' Mac said. 'I've found a sort of link but it's all a bit tenuous at the moment. I'll fill you in once I've followed a few things up, if that's okay. How's the exercise going?'

Andy raised his eyes to the ceiling and checked his watch again.

'I've got a meeting at one thirty and from then on it's all about this bloody exercise. I'm afraid you won't be able to reach me until after it's over. Toni Woodgate's in charge until I get back if you need anything. I really could have done without it with everything we've got on at the moment. The wife isn't too happy about it either as it means that I'll be away all over Easter.'

'Shall we meet up in the middle of next week? I'll bring you up to date then,' Mac said.

'Yes, and hopefully over a pint or two. I'll need a drink when it's all over.'

After Andy had gone Mac got himself another coffee and thought about his next steps.

He checked his emails on his tablet and found that he'd missed one that had come in yesterday evening. It was the personnel files belonging to Dr. Christodoulou and Dr. Soulis. He decided to go home, get comfortable, and open it up on his laptop.

He made a pot of coffee and put on some Vivaldi. Then he opened the first of the PDF documents and read.

Dr. Kostas Christodoulou, born in Athens in 1959, so knocking on for sixty now. He'd been employed at the Medical School for the last nine years or so as the Departmental Research Tutor for Post-Graduate Medicine. His previous CV looked very impressive. His sick days were below average and his appraisals were well above. He had several previous jobs, the first was in Athens and the rest in different parts of the US. Mac noticed that one of them was at the famous Mayo Clinic and was impressed.

Dr. Lena Soulis, born in Kalamata in 1986, so she was around thirty. She'd been employed by the School ever since she'd graduated as a doctor and was now working as part of the Consultancy Team, whatever that was. Her appraisals were brilliant and she had an unblemished work record. No sick days.

Nothing in any of the documents gave Mac anything to be excited about but he'd follow it up anyway. He rang and arranged to meet them at the Medical School.

Dr. Christodoulou first, as he said he'd be free in an hour, and then Dr. Soulis at four thirty.

As he drove to the Medical School, he tried to think of what he should tell them. If he told them the truth then they'd probably think that he was crazy. He would have to get another story together.

He got lost again and only just made his first appointment.

Dr. Christodoulou was of medium height, with a square sort of face, his black hair greying at the sides. He wore his white coat with an air of sure authority about him. If this man told you that he was a doctor then you would absolutely believe him.

He shut the door to his office and sat down.

'So, what's this all about?' he asked.

Mac licked his lips.

'I'm afraid that I can't go into details but we're looking for someone who visited the Records Office in Hertford recently. We believe he may be a doctor and of Greek origin.'

The doctor looked hugely sceptical at Mac's words.

'Mr. Maguire you're using some very fuzzy words there. I know it seems to be open season on Greeks at the moment but you've not told me anything yet that might make me want to co-operate.'

There was silence for a moment while Mac thought. He'd come up with a story but the sceptical way the man in front of him was looking at him made him think again.

He made his decision. He'd take the easiest path. He told the doctor everything just as it had happened.

This time it was the doctor's turn to be silent.

'Okay,' he finally said. 'I can see your logic, tenuous though it might be. How can I help?'

'I just need to exclude you from the investigation. Can I?'

'You can. I had nothing to do with these robberies,' the doctor said.

'Thank you.'

Mac absolutely believed him. He got up and made for the door.

It was halfway open when the doctor said, 'But then again, if I was involved, isn't that exactly what I'd say anyway?'

Mac looked over his shoulder to see a big grin on the doctor's face. His knew that his leg was being severely pulled.

He managed to grab a coffee while he waited for his next appointment. Dr. Soulis said she'd meet him in the coffee shop so, thankfully, he didn't have to move again.

Dr. Soulis was slim, dark haired, dark skinned and entirely lovely. A waft of her perfume made Mac go slightly weak at the knees and think of things that he hadn't thought of for quite some time.

Be professional, he reminded himself.

He decided to do the same as he'd done previously and just tell her the whole story.

'That's really strange isn't it?' she said. 'I mean some-one breaking in and just stealing chocolate. There's a famous burglar in Athens who steals chocolate but I've never heard of it over here.'

Mac was glad that she'd reminded him. He'd nearly forgotten about the Chocolate Thief.

'So, you can't tell me anything that might help?'

She shook her head. Perhaps he was on the wrong track after all.

As she stood up to go Mac said, 'It's a pity that there's only you and Dr. Christodoulou who are from Greece. I was so sure.'

She sat down again. Her face was thoughtful.

'There was another one, another doctor from Greece.'

Mac looked up quickly.

'Really? But I was told that there were only two doctors from Greece employed by the school.'

'Well that may still be right. The doctor I'm thinking of was on attachment from Athens University so I'm not sure that it would count as being employed. He was here for a couple of years or so on a scholarship doing some research on rheumatic diseases. He was very good and very cute too,' she said with a sweet smile.

Right then Mac was slightly sad that his 'cute' days were over, if he'd ever had any that was.

She wrote down his name, Dr. Nikos Nicolaou. Mac looked at it as though he might be able to tease some meaning out of the letters themselves.

Perhaps he could after all. He had a sudden thought.

'Dr. Soulis, how long have you been in the UK, if you don't mind me asking?'

'No, I don't mind,' she replied. 'I've been here since I was fifteen. My family moved here when my father got a job at a university in London.'

'So, you've been here for quite some time, however, I'm wondering about Dr. Nicolaou. If he'd not been here all that long then it's possible that he might have been a little homesick. If he'd have wanted to meet other Greek people, is there anywhere near here where he could have done that?'

She gave it some thought.

'Yes, there is somewhere. There's a Greek Orthodox church not too far away. I'm not sure how religious Dr. Nicolaou was but I know that they organise a lot of social events.'

She got her phone out and found the website. Mac made a note of the web address.

'Is there anything else you can think of that might help?' Mac asked, hoping there was so he could have a little more of her time.

'I'm sorry,' she said with a little shrug of the shoulders.

They shook hands and then she left leaving only her perfume behind.

Mac wondered at himself feeling any attraction to a woman. He'd not felt anything remotely like that since Nora died and he couldn't help feeling more than a little guilty.

He suddenly realised the time. It was now four forty five and he had to get to Mrs. Cresswell's office as soon as possible. Of course, he got lost again and, when he finally found it, he parked at an angle and left the green Almera unlocked. He had no time.

He hobbled into the building as fast as he could and breathlessly asked the receptionist if Mrs. Cresswell was in. He was lucky, she was planning to leave in a few minutes.

She didn't look all that happy to be helping him so late in the day but Mac didn't care. The good side of it was that she didn't cavil at his request and was only too happy to load the doctor's file onto his tablet as quickly as she could. She also sent a copy to Andy.

Mac sat in his car and read the file on his tablet.

Dr. Nikos Nicolaou, who was twenty seven years old, was a graduate of Athens University and was studying at the school having won a medical scholarship. He specialised in rheumatic diseases and the sabbatical was part of his research into the prevalence of these diseases in Central Greece. He was going to compare the rates of these diseases compared to those in Britain. His appraisals were uniformly excellent, all rated as 'above expectations'.

His next of kin was a Mrs. Sofia Nicolaou and it gave her address. Agiou Athiris! Mac all but cheered. He now knew that he was definitely on the right track.

It also gave a UK address, a flat in Hatfield, and, unfortunately, very little else. Mac sat back and thought for a moment.

Before he drove off Mac looked up the church on his tablet. He fed the address into the satnav and was surprised that it would take him less than fifteen minutes to drive there from where he was.

As it was even nearer, he first visited the flat in Hatfield. It was now being leased by an elderly couple. They'd never met the previous tenant but they said that the neighbours talked highly of him. They gave him the name of the letting agents. Mac would look them up later if he needed to. He tried the neighbours but, as they weren't in, he decided to go straight to the church.

The Church of the Four Evangelists looked like any Victorian English parish church on the outside. It was built of grey stone and had a peaked roof with a little bell tower on top. Inside though it was totally different as the church was richly decorated and glittered with gold. Mac's eyes were especially drawn to a golden screen covering the wall behind the altar. On the screen four men were sumptuously depicted, each of who were holding an open book. The walls were also covered with icons. Mac stopped and looked closely at one of a Madonna and child. It was beautiful.

'It's not real I'm afraid,' a voice with a London accent said.

Mac turned to see a man in his mid-thirties, dark skinned, black haired and bearded. He was simply dressed in black trousers and a white open necked shirt. He smiled at Mac.

'Can I help you?' he asked.

'I'm looking for the parish priest.'

The man's smile broadened.

'You've found him.'

Mac wasn't quite sure what he'd been expecting but this young, confident Londoner was definitely not it. Mac showed him his warrant card.

'I'm Father Joseph Stavrou,' he said as they shook hands. 'Let's find somewhere a bit more comfortable.'

Mac followed the priest and the aroma of coffee into a little office.

'Coffee?' the priest asked.

'Yes please.'

It was proper coffee too, strong and intense.

Father Joseph cut to the chase.

'So, how can I help the police?'

'I'm looking for a Dr. Nikos Nicolaou. Do you know him?'

The priest thought for quite a while.

'Yes, yes I think I do but I haven't seen him for a while. I think he worked at the Medical School in Hatfield. Is that the one you're asking about?'

Mac cheered inwardly again.

'Yes, that's him. When was the last time you saw him?'

Father Joseph gave it some thought.

'Well he never came to mass that much, I don't think he was all that religious really, but we used to see him at some of our social events. I remember him telling me that he enjoyed meeting up with other Greeks as he was missing home so much. I don't remember seeing him recently though, probably not for some months I should think. Can I ask what this is all about?'

'I'm just making some enquiries,' Mac said non-committedly. 'Did he have any friends in your congregation, anyone he might think of staying with?'

He could see the cogs going around in the young priest's mind. A decision was made and it went against Mac. The open, animated expression on his face was replaced with something more closed off.

'I'm sorry but no. I didn't know him all that well.'

Mac knew that there was no point in pushing it.

'Can you at least try and get a message to him, if he's still around that is?' Mac said as he pulled a Garden City Detective card from his pocket.

Father Joseph looked a little puzzled.

'I thought that you were a policeman?'

'I'm a retired policeman, currently helping the police with this case. Can you tell Dr. Nicolaou that, if he wants to meet, I can meet him as a private detective rather than a policeman if he'd prefer that.'

Mac could see that the priest was still reluctant.

'Look what harm can it do? Just tell Dr. Nicolaou that I know what happened in Agiou Athiris in 1947. I'd be really grateful if you could do that. Please?'

Mac wasn't totally sure that he'd swayed the young priest but all he could do now was hope.

As he drove back home along the motorway, he tried to think of what else he could do to push the case along but nothing came to mind. He looked at the clock. He was surprised to find that it was nearly seven. When he got home, he made two calls, one to Tim to confirm the pub, and the other to Eileen, his favourite taxi driver.

By seven thirty he was comfortably seated at table thirteen in the Magnets. Tim was happy. He'd bought a piece of furniture he'd noticed in a junk shop in North London. He reckoned that with a little bit of 'TLC', as he called it, it would be worth ten times what he paid. Tim loved a bargain.

Mac brought him up to date with the case. He thought his friend still looked a bit dubious about his lead.

'I suppose you know what you're doing though,' Tim conceded.

Mac suddenly wasn't so sure. A photo being moved and something mysterious that had happened in a Greek town seventy years ago, it all seemed a bit far-fetched right at that moment.

Then his phone rang. He had a message.

'Meet us at the church tomorrow morning at ten. Only you or there will be no meeting.'

There was no name but Mac knew who it was. Mac smiled a broad smile as he showed the message to Tim.

'Ah well, perhaps you haven't lost your touch after all then. Another pint?'

Chapter Twelve

Three days to Easter

Mac slept fitfully. Whether this was due to the pain or his excitement at what the next day might bring he wasn't quite sure.

By six thirty he was showered and shaved. He had a quick breakfast of coffee and toast as he watched the birds fluttering around the feeders. His back grumbled at him for a while but he ignored it.

Without much hope he put Dr. Nikos Nicolaou in Google and was quite surprised when it spat out two relevant results.

The first was a PDF abstract of a medical paper 'Epidemiology of Rheumatic Diseases: Incidence and Outcomes of Rheumatic Diseases in Rural Greece'. Mac scanned the abstract but couldn't make much of it. The other result proved to be more interesting. It was in Greek so Mac had to get the page translated.

It was from a local news website. The first article was entitled 'Big scandal at local hospital' and Mac read it carefully. However, it made no mention of a Dr. Nicolaou. He had to go down the page before he found another article entitled 'Local boy wins scholarship'. The article was three and a half years old.

'Local boy Dr. Nikos Nicolaou has won a scholarship to study in England. The scholarship will allow him to work at a medical school there and learn more about his speciality, epidemiology. Dr. Nicolaou said that 'He hoped that he'd be able to use his studies to make the lives of people who suffer from rheumatic diseases a little easier in the years to come.'

There was a small photo. Mac looked at it for some time. It showed a young man in a classic pose, the white doctor's coat with the stethoscope draped around his neck. The young man was tall, dark skinned and had black curly hair. He was smiling and not just with his mouth. It somehow wasn't what Mac had been expecting.

He still had a little time so he decided to re-read Edward Chappell's journal. He wanted to be sure that he had it all in his head for his meeting with the doctor.

He left early and was glad he'd done so as the traffic crawled at walking pace past Stevenage. Even so he was still parked outside the church a good half hour before the due time. He waited and watched but no-one came out or went in. At nine fifty eight he walked towards the church, hoping that Dr. Nicolaou had gotten there early and that it wasn't going to be a wild goose chase.

He was met by Father Joseph as he entered the church.

'Are you alone?' the young priest asked.

'I am.'

'Follow me then.'

Mac noticed that he kept looking behind him as he walked. Perhaps the priest didn't quite trust Mac.

'Here,' Father Joseph said as he held open a door.

Mac found his heart was beating faster as he entered. He so wanted to know what this was all about.

Inside there was a small coffee shop. Two men were sitting at a table. They both stood up when Mac entered the room. One was the young doctor, who looked quite anxious, the other was an old man in his late sixties or seventies. He had grey hair and a large grey moustache. The resemblance to the young doctor was inescapable.

The old man waved at a chair, 'Join us, please,' he said in accented English.

Mac sat down.

'I am Professor Dr. Nikos Nicolaou,' the old man said.

Now Mac was confused.

'I thought he was Dr. Nikos Nicolaou,' he said pointing at the young man.

The old man smiled.

'Yes, you're right. He's a real doctor though whereas my doctorate was only in history. Also, in my family we tend to use the same personal names. There has been a Nikos Nicolaou in each generation of our family going back centuries.'

Mac understood this concept well. If you got a large number of Irishmen together and yelled out just four first names it would pretty much cover everyone there.

'You say that you know what happened in our town in 1947. Is that right?' the old man asked.

'I lied,' Mac admitted. 'But I really want to learn what happened and I've got a feeling that you know all about it. By the way where's the Chocolate Thief now, has he gone back home?'

The two men looked at each other in some wonder.

'How did you know about him?' the young one asked.

'From an article I read right at the start of the case. I've come across quite a few burglars in my time who liked to leave their signature behind. The only one I found who stole chocolate worked in Athens. Has he gone home?'

'Yes, he said that finding the old lady nearly dead like that was like an omen or something. He caught the next flight home,' the young doctor said.

'The lady he found told me that he said something. 'Hockey' she thought it was.'

'He said 'Οχι'. It means 'no' in Greek.'

This now made perfect sense to Mac. It's exactly the word someone might use when they break in only to find an old lady who had fallen down the stairs.

'Is he family?' Mac asked.

'My cousin,' the young Nikos replied. 'He's a designer by trade but when he couldn't get any work he started stealing. He only steals from those who can afford it though.'

'Tell him he's very good. So, what is it exactly that you want from Mr. Llewellyn-fforbes?'

Once again, the two men looked at each other.

'You may not know what happened in 1947 but you seem to know just about everything else,' the older Nikos said.

'So, tell me then. What happened in Agiou Athiris in 1947?' Mac asked bluntly.

The old man spread his hands out on the table. Mac could see that they were shaking slightly.

'I will but first I need to tell you what started all of this off. Is that okay?'

Mac nodded. The old man told his story.

'This is going to sound a little crazy, it still does to me if I'm honest, but three months ago I had a dream. In it I saw a man running out of a burning building. He was carrying something which he then covered in a blanket and put in the back of a jeep. He then drove off. That was it. Not much really but, at the time, the dream seemed very powerful and very real. Even so I just dismissed it. Then three days later I had it again except this time I knew it wasn't a dream but a memory of something that had really happened.

It took me a while but eventually it came back to me. I must have been only nine or ten at the time and there was trouble in the town. My mother had warned me not to go anywhere near the square but I couldn't help myself. I hid in an alleyway and poked my head around the corner to see what was going on. I couldn't see much but I could hear well enough. I heard the crowd shouting 'Leave the priest alone' and then I saw flames coming from the church. The shouting from the square grew louder and the police that had been surrounding the church ran towards the square. I then saw a man in a brown uniform walking away from the square. I knew that uniform, he was a British soldier. He stopped and looked at the back door of the church. He then broke it open using the sole of his boot.

Smoke belched out of the door and I was amazed to see the soldier run into the building. I saw orange flames lick around the door and I feared that he might be dead when he suddenly ran out of the doorway and into the street. His face and uniform were black with smoke. I caught a glimpse of the thing he'd carried out. It was an icon, our icon, the town's most treasured possession, Our Lady of Agiou Athiris. He wrapped it in a blanket and drove off.

I remembered telling my mother about it at the time but she made me swear never to tell anyone. She said that God had saved the icon and it would come home in its own time. She told me to forget all about it and I suppose I did just that. Why I dreamed about it some seventy years later I still have no idea.

The third time I had the dream was even more powerful than the second. I, like my father, am a man of the left and I'm not at all religious. Yet, when I woke up, I knew that I had to do something about it. As mad as it all sounded, I told my young grandson Nikos here and, for some reason, he believed me.'

Old and young Nikos looked at each other with great affection.

'So, we started looking for the soldier who had saved the icon,' old Nikos said.

'Or stole it perhaps?' Mac suggested.

The old man shrugged.

'Perhaps but all I knew was that we had to find it.'

'Why?' Mac asked.

He was totally intrigued by the whole thing now.

'Hope,' the old man said. 'I've lived a long time but I've never known it worse than it is now. I came back to Agiou Athiris from Athens to retire some years ago and what I found disgusted me. Almost half the town was out of work after two manufacturing plants had closed. It was bad enough for the old but I feared most of all for our young people. At my age I've known prosperity and

112

some good times but for the young it is truly desperate. There's no work for them, no hope. They have nothing to look forward to in life. This austerity has ground us all down but the young worst of all.'

'So, you thought that finding the icon might change things?' Mac asked.

The old man smiled and shook his head.

'I told you it was crazy. I can't see how it can change anything really but for some reason I have to find it, I have to.'

Mac didn't doubt his sincerity.

'Go on,' he prompted.

'So, we found it hard going at first. All we knew was that he was a British soldier in Agiou Athiris in 1947. I didn't know if he was an officer or anything just that he was a soldier and what his face looked like. Nikos did all the research, eventually finding the journal in the museum. That gave us the names and then he was able to find out who their children were.'

'Whose idea was it to break into their homes?' Mac asked.

Young Nikos put his hand up.

'I didn't think it was very practical to just knock on doors and ask whether or not a relative of theirs had stolen a valuable painting seventy years ago. So, I contacted my cousin who thought I'd gone mad but, as he likes mad things, he was all for it.'

'So, what was he doing, taking photos of any pictures of men in uniform?' Mac asked.

'Yes, except for the Pegrams,' the doctor said. 'He couldn't find any photos so he downloaded everything on their tablet and we found the photos there.'

Mac thought it was all very clever.

'What made you do them in the order you did?'

'We just put the names in a hat and drew them out at random,' young Nikos replied. 'It was our bad luck that we had to wait until the sixth one before we knew we had the right man.'

'Whose idea was it to do the last one in Henlow?'

'That was mine too,' young Nikos said. 'I thought someone might catch on if the burglaries finished with the Llewellyn-fforbes one.'

'That was clever too,' Mac said. 'So, now that you know who took the icon, what were you planning to do next?'

'To be honest we had no clear idea,' old Nikos admitted. 'We know that the icon hadn't been sold and, as far as we could tell, that it wasn't in a museum either. It's very special, different to any other icon. We therefore knew that Mr. Llewellyn-fforbes must still have it. But what do you do, knock on the front door and ask him if he could return a valuable painting that his father took seventy years ago?'

Mac gave it some very serious thought.

'I think that's exactly what you should do. If you're up for it that is?' Mac asked.

'We've come a long way and we've spent a lot of time looking for our icon. We're absolutely up for it,' old Nikos stated.

Mac left the room and noticed Father Joseph hovering outside. He looked worried.

'It's okay Father, you can relax. Go and speak to them.'

He phoned Monty Llewellyn-fforbes and, luckily, he was in.

'I was about to go out in a minute though. Is it important?' Monty asked.

'It's very important,' Mac confirmed without saying anything more.

Monty said that he'd wait for him.

Half an hour later Monty himself opened the door. He showed some surprise that Mac was accompanied but waved at them all to follow him inside.

He led them into the living room and waved at a sofa.

'So, what's this all about then?' Monty asked when everyone had sat down.

'It's about the break-in,' Mac explained.

'Do they know who did it?' Monty said pointing at the two men.

'No, they're the ones who did it.'

Monty's face started to grow red. He stood up and waved his stick.

'Is this a joke? If it is then it's in bloody poor taste,' he exclaimed.

Mac thought he better explain quickly before someone got hurt.

'Monty, please sit down and listen. If you still want to hit anyone afterwards you can start with me.'

Somewhat reluctantly he sat down again.

'Please let this man tell you his story,' Mac asked.

He nodded at old Nikos.

'My name is Nikos Nicolaou and I had a dream...'

Old Nikos told his story exactly as he had to Mac earlier. At the end Monty was silent for a few moments.

'So, you're saying that my father stole this painting?' he said his face getting red again.

'Not necessarily stole it but perhaps he...' old Nikos said trying to think of another explanation. He couldn't think of one so he never finished the sentence.

The room fell silent, so silent that they could all hear the sound of the front door being opened and steps heading in their direction. The door opened and Helena appeared.

'Hello Monty, I'm back...'

She stopped dead when she saw who was in the room.

'Oh, I'm sorry, I didn't know you had company...'

Mac watched her as her eyes scanned the room. When they fell on young Nikos, he could see that she was really surprised.

Young Nikos stood up and said, 'Dr. Biggerstaff!'

'Dr. Nicolaou!' she replied her face suddenly becoming flushed.

'Helena, you've come just in time. Can you do me a favour?' Monty asked.

'Of course,' she replied.

'You know where all the keys are kept. Can you find the one for my father's room then go in and see if you can find a painting in there? It might be wrapped up. How big is it?' Monty asked.

Old Nikos demonstrated the size using his hands.

Not all that big then, Mac thought.

Helena went to look for the painting.

'If your painting's anywhere it will be there,' Monty stated with some certainty.

'How can you be so sure?' Mac asked.

'Because we'd have found it by now if it had been anywhere else. I never cleared my father's room out after he died.'

'Why was that?' Mac asked.

'Just never got around to it somehow,' Monty said gruffly.

He stood up and walked towards the window. He stood there looking out of the window until some fifteen minutes later when Helena came into the room. She was carrying a package.

'I found this at the back of his wardrobe,' she said.

She laid it on the table. It was wrapped in brown paper and string. She went off and returned with some scissors.

She cut the string and pulled back the paper. It was brittle and bits of it cracked and fell off onto the table. There was a further level of wrapping, something that looked like chamois leather. Helena pulled it back and the contents were revealed.

It wasn't a painting but a photograph of a young woman. From her hairstyle and clothes Mac reckoned it must have been taken in the forties.

'That's my mother!' Monty exclaimed.

'Here,' Helena said.

She gave Monty a thick envelope. It had his name on the front in faded ink – 'Monty'. Monty patted his pockets.

'Helena can you read it? I can't find my glasses.'

She opened the envelope and pulled out several sheets of paper. She started reading…

'My dear Monty,

You will have found this while you were cleaning out my room. I am dead now but I hope that you can help me with something, something I should have done while I was alive. I'm afraid that I have to admit that your father has been something of a coward.'

Everyone instinctively looked at Monty. He looked shocked. Helena continued.

'I need to tell you about what happened to me in Greece. Perhaps I should have told you all this a long time ago but hopefully you will understand why in a moment.

We were sent to Greece in 1943, mainly I think as I was fluent in Ancient Greek and the top brass thought that was near enough. We fought alongside a group of Partisans led by the Nicolaou brothers.'

Now everyone turned and looked at old Nikos.

'Read on,' he pleaded.

'The Partisans were amongst the best men I'd ever met. I didn't agree with their politics but, then again, I don't suppose they agreed with mine either. We got to know all them very well and, for me, they were like my brothers, most especially the two Nicolaous, Nikos and Michalis. We called them Nicky and Mickey which they loved. They said it made them sound like American gangsters.'

Mac noticed a tear rolling down old Nikos' face.

'When we were in the mountains, we had a lot of time to talk. The brothers especially liked to hear about the history of their people so I used to tell them stories taken from the likes of Heroditus, Thucydides and Xenophon.

117

They loved hearing about the great battles that the Ancient Greeks had fought. Mickey especially loved to hear about Themistocles and the great sea battle of Salamis.'

Everyone turned to look at old Nikos who suddenly appeared to be somewhat agitated.

'Please read on,' he said again.

'When the war ended, we were all so happy but I'm afraid that it didn't last long. In December of 1944 I was invited to Athens by the General and there I witnessed the most appalling scenes, something I have never forgotten and God knows I've tried. The British and Americans, in their great wisdom, had put the Greek thugs who had sided with the Nazis back in power and ordered the Partisans to disarm. Of course, they said no and two hundred thousand people marched in Athens to protest at what they were being asked to do.

We shouldn't have been surprised when the Greek thugs opened fire and shot into the crowd killing many of their own citizens. All of them were unarmed. We should have shot the thugs down right there and then but we didn't because we were now on their side. So, we just stood by with our guns and tanks and watched. It sickened me then and it still does now all these years later.

I was then ordered by the General to hunt down all the Partisans in my area. Arrest them if possible, kill them if not. As I drove back to the town of Agiou Athiris, I will admit that I wept. I explained the situation to my men who didn't seem any more enthusiastic about turning against our friends than I was. So, we had a sort of phoney war for a while. We'd pretend to try and hunt them down and the Partisans would pretend to be fighting us. While we were with the Colonel and the local security forces, Nazis sympathisers to a man, Nicky and Mickey would fire at us but over our heads. I knew they could have picked an eye and hit it if they'd have wanted to.

And so it went on. Our hands were bound and, as much as we might have wanted to, we could do nothing to help our friends except to do nothing. In the end, all I and the men could do was pray for it to be over, we just wanted to go home and get away from all the madness. Then something happened that forced our hand.

More by luck than anything else the security forces stumbled on a group of Partisans and captured them. Among them were Nicky and Mickey. They took them to the local jail where they beat them quite savagely. Then some of the Greek soldiers went to a bar where a couple of my men were drinking and boasted about what they'd done. They said that they'd never live to see a trial as their Colonel was planning on taking them into the woods and killing them all. One Partisan, one bullet they said.

My men didn't take this well and it ended up in a fight. One I'm glad to say that my men won. I was more than happy to pay for the damage.

However, we now had a decision to make and I'm more than proud that all of the men who had fought with the Partisans stood together on this. We've had some new recruits join us but we thought it best to keep them out of this. It wasn't their fight.

We all agreed that we needed to break our friends out of prison. It wasn't hard. The guards were both drunks so a couple of bottles of retsina laced with Benny's home-brewed poteen did the trick. They were asleep in no time. All we had to do was go in, open the cells and lead our friends out of a side entrance into our truck. Once they were well out of town my Sergeant, an explosives expert, blew down the outer wall of the prison. We hoped that the security forces would think that they'd just escaped and were still somewhere in the town. By the time they visited our barracks my men were all back in their beds.

The General himself came and tore a strip off me and my men. He had a good idea that we were in it up to our necks. The men followed my advice and said nothing.

There was no evidence against us but, as the General said we were no longer to be trusted, we were to be sent home. He said that we should all be ashamed. I must admit that I felt little shame and I don't think any of my men did either. After he'd gone, we had a sort of party. We were all so glad to be going home.

Now we come to the real point of this letter. The day before we were due to go home the Colonel invited us to the main square where we had to witness the beating of the local priest. It was vile. He was not a young man and the way the Colonel obviously enjoyed it was sickening. He looked at me from time to time. I daresay he wished it was me and not the priest that was feeling the leather of his men's boots.

Then he committed a great sin, I can only call it that. He stood by as the church burnt down. The Colonel laughed at me. I could hear the crowd shouting and some of them tried to get to the church to put out the fire. The Colonel stopped them. I couldn't watch and walked away. The soldiers surrounding the church all ran into the square and then I saw the back door. I must have gone a little mad I suppose because I kicked down the door and ran into the flames. I can still feel their heat on my skin as I write this letter. I should have died that day but I didn't. Only God knows why.

I came out of the church with something valuable, perhaps the most valuable thing in the town of Agiou Athiris, an icon. Not in terms of money, although it must be worth a lot, but because it has been the centre of religious devotion in that town for many centuries. They used to process the icon all around the town every Easter. An old man once called it 'the Heartbeat of Agiou Athiris'. I saved it.

I threw it in the back of my jeep and drove off. No-one saw me. The problem was I didn't know what to do with it next. The only men I could have trusted were all in the mountains and on the run. I had no time to arrange anything as we were all going home the next day. So, I took it back with me. I tried to keep in touch with my old friends but it was hard. Then a couple of years later I heard the news. Nicky and Mickey were dead, shot by the miserable bastards we'd handed the town over to. I cried the day I heard that news and I despaired for the country whose history I'd studied so long and for which I'd fought so hard.

I thought no more of the icon. If I thought of that then I would have to remember the way my friends, no my brothers, had died. I couldn't bear it.

Now I near death and, after all these years, the icon has suddenly come back into my mind. So, I must admit to my cowardice and ask you to do what I could not. Please return the icon to Agiou Athiris, to where it rightfully belongs. I have heard that Mickey had a son, search him out. If he is half the man his father was then he will do what is right.

My dear Monty, I am sorry to burden you with this but I know you will do what I couldn't and help me rest. I have been proud of you every day since the day you were born and I still am. I could not have wished for a better son,

Your loving father

Harry'

There was stunned silence for a minute or so. It was broken by old Nikos.

'Your father, he was no coward,' he stated with certainty.

'How do you know?' Monty asked, his eyes brimming with tears.

'I didn't know who your father really was until she read that letter out. My father, Mickey as your father used to call him, used to sneak back home for a night now and again. To be with my mother I suppose. He used to tell us stories and the ones we loved most were those that 'The Historian' had told him. He told us that every time he heard one of these stories it made him feel a foot taller to be a Greek. He said that we should all be very proud of what our small country had given to the world. I became a historian myself because of those stories. He said that The Historian was a very brave man who had saved his and my uncle's life many times when they were fighting the Germans. He said he was a true brother and a friend of Greece. Your father was no coward.'

Monty stood up and offered old Nikos his hand. Nikos ignored it and hugged Monty. To Mac's surprise Monty hugged back. Nikos then kissed Monty on both cheeks. Mac wasn't totally surprised when Monty didn't kiss him back.

'So, is that the icon?' Monty asked, pointing to the picture of his mother.

'Yes,' old Nikos replied. 'I recognize the frame and you can see here, on the lower right-hand corner, it's all worn away. We used to pray before the icon and then kiss it just there. You can see centuries of kisses right there.'

'May I?' young Nikos asked.

He produced a small pocket knife and gently removed the glass. He then reverently gave the photo to Monty. Below the photo was another layer of thin chamois leather. Nikos removed this.

It was as though the sun had just risen in Monty's living room. Mac had to look away, he was blinded.

He looked back and young Nikos had angled the frame so the light wouldn't dazzle them. Mac's eyes were immediately drawn to the lustrous gold that formed the background of the painting, then next to the deep blue colour of the woman's robes, a darker blue in the folds and shadows, and then to the baby she cradled in her arms. He smiled and looked straight out of the painting. His head was haloed in gold and he made a sign of peace with one hand. Then last of all to the woman's face. Once there, Mac found that he was entranced.

She didn't look out at him, she was looking down at the child that she held so tenderly in her arms. She was not beautiful but the way she had been painted made her transcend beauty. She had a smile on her face but it was a sad one. She looked with loving tenderness at her son and it was as though she already knew of the pain and torture that this beautiful child would have to go through in his short life. The eyes showed the true depth of her sadness and, as if to confirm this, on one cheek a golden tear was eternally suspended.

Mac thought that it was one of the most beautiful and most heart-breaking things that he'd ever seen.

'We've found her,' old Nikos said as the tears flowed down his cheeks.

His grandson embraced him and held him until the tears stopped.

'She is beautiful indeed but what now?' Monty asked being practical.

'I suppose that we should notify our governments?' young Nikos suggested somewhat tentatively.

This suggestion didn't go down too well with Monty.

'What? Then you'd all have to go down to the National Gallery to see it. It would stay there for the next fifty years or so while they bicker about it who owns it. No that won't do, not at all.' He seemed to have a thought. 'Didn't my father say that you used to have a procession at Easter?'

Old Nikos nodded.

'Well, you've got three days or so to get it back then, haven't you?' Monty said with a big smile.

Both old and young Nikos smiled too. Mac was totally amazed. Somehow it wasn't what he'd expected from Monty.

'How will you do it?' Monty asked.

'We know someone at the Embassy here in London who might be able get it out of England in the diplomatic bag,' young Nikos replied.

'Another cousin?' Mac asked with a smile.

'No but he comes from our town. It's as important to him as it is to us.'

'What will you tell them?' Monty asked.

Mac could see he was concerned in case anyone might mistake his father's motives.

'Yes,' old Nikos said as he rubbed his chin. 'We need a story.' He thought for a while. 'What about this?'

He told them about his idea. Mac thought it was brilliant and, with a few tweaks, they all agreed that it would do.

'Well, you'd better get going then, hadn't you?' Monty said.

Old Nikos hugged Monty again and young Nikos did the same. Old Nikos shook Helena's hand with feeling. Young Nikos shook her hand too and seemed to take his time about it.

'Come on, we must go,' old Nikos eventually said with urgency.

Young Nikos tore himself away and picked up the icon. Before he left the room, he stopped and looked back. Helena had turned around and didn't see the expression of longing on his face.

The room must have been silent for at least a couple of minutes. They all looked at each other as though to ask, 'Did that really happen?'

Monty cleared his throat.

'Well, who'd have thought that then?'

'Monty, would you like a drink?' Helena asked.

'Yes, a whisky and make it a bloody stiff one please.'

Mac declined as he was driving.

'Yes, who'd have thought that?' he said again. 'Mr. Maguire, I'd like to thank you for your part in all this.

I've been thinking about my father quite a lot recently, now I think I know why.'

'You did the right thing Monty. I was very, very proud of what you did just now,' Mac said.

'It was nothing really. How could I worry about giving away something that I never knew I had? I just hope it does them some good, I really do.'

'But you did find something of value tonight, didn't you?'

Monty's eyes brimmed again.

'Yes, and it was something more valuable to me than all the paintings in the world.'

Helena came back with two glasses. She gave one to Monty.

'If you both don't mind, I think I'd like to read this again myself,' Monty said as he picked up his father's letter.

Helena and Mac left him in peace.

'I'll show you out,' she offered.

'That letter has really affected Monty,' Mac stated.

'Yes, he and his father were very close. I think it always pained him a little that his father would never tell him about the war though.'

'And now he has and from the grave at that.'

Helena was about to open the door when Mac asked her a question. One he knew he had to get the answer to before he left.

'You and Dr. Nicolaou, you've met before, haven't you?'

Helena took her hand off the door latch, looked up to the ceiling and then sat down on the nearby stairs.

'Yes, we've met before. We met just the once and it lasted exactly twenty eight minutes. We both attended the same Medical School. I was finishing off my studies, he was a researcher. We must have been there together for at least a year but we never bumped into each other until his leaving party. That's strange, isn't it?

Anyway, I went to his leaving party to give a friend something. She said that she'd be definitely there. So, I dropped in on my way to work, the night shift at the local hospital. My friend wasn't there but Dr. Nicolaou was. We talked for twenty eight minutes and then I had to go. I felt that there was a real connection between us, something that I can't explain. Anyway, he was flying back to Greece for a year's sabbatical so I figured that it wasn't meant to be. I've thought about him since though.'

She shrugged her shoulders.

'And now you meet again,' Mac said.

'Yes, and he's flying back to bloody Greece again, isn't he?' she said, the frustration clear in her voice.

Helena seemed to be quite upset about someone she'd only met twice and fleetingly at that. Mac gave it some thought.

'Well at least you know where he lives. You know I'd bet that, with a little persuasion, Monty would love to go to Agiou Athiris is a week or two and see where his father had spent so many years during the war. Of course, he's old now and I guess that he'll need someone to help him...'

Helena jumped up. She had a big smile on her face. She gave Mac a kiss on the cheek.

'Thank you, Mr. Maguire. I think that's an absolutely excellent idea.'

As he drove home Mac wondered how it would all turn out. Would the icon really restore some hope to a town battered by the storms of austerity? Would Helena get to meet young Nikos again and, if she did, how would it turn out? Mac would just have to wait and see.

He looked at his watch. It was only two o'clock.

He rang Tim who was all up for knocking off early and meeting him at the Magnets.

Mac was glad. He had a whopper of a story to tell him.

Chapter Thirteen

Friday – Two days to Easter

Mac woke up quite late that morning. He'd gone to bed fairly early so he reckoned that he must have needed the sleep.

He sat on the edge of the bed trying to get his mind to focus. Somehow yesterday's events seemed more like one of the surreal lucid dreams that he had from time to time than a real memory. He suddenly remembered that he was supposed to be meeting with Jimmy Carmichael and he was glad that he had a few hours free before he had to do that. He said a little prayer and then stood up and checked his pain levels. They weren't too bad. He showered and shaved and, after some coffee and toast, he went to the cemetery to tell Nora everything that had happened.

It was nearly mid-day by the time he'd finished. He decided that he might as well do some research on Thomas Pierson until it was time to go and pick up Jimmy.

Born in St. Ippolyts, the young Pierson was taken to New York as a teenager when his family moved there. He attended Columbia University, where his father was a professor, and he did a degree in Fine Arts. Pierson was quoted as saying that his real education was hanging out with people like Warhol and Rauschenberg in the sixties New York art scene. He found a photo showing a young Warhol dressed in a leather jacket and sunglasses. It was taken in the famous Factory and, in the background, a young long-haired Pierson could be seen leaning against a wall. He also found a portrait of Warhol that Pierson had painted in the early seventies before he left New York for good. It was now hanging in the New York Metropolitan Museum of Art. He read that, even though he hung out with Warhol, Pierson's work could never be classified as Pop Art. It was something else entirely. No-one knows why but he suddenly left America and went back to the family home in St. Ippolyts in the mid-seventies. He never left England again. He painted many local scenes in Hertfordshire and also in Devon but his most sought-after works were his 'memory paintings' of New York. All were done in St. Ippolyts but they were recognisably those of a New York that no longer existed.

Mac looked hard at a number of Pierson's paintings but he wasn't sure what he made of them. It was as though he was looking at a scene through some sort of distorting lens.

He came across a recent article that pointed out that Pierson's popularity was only likely to grow now that he was dead. With no more works possible those remaining pieces would become even more valuable. The author illustrated this point by noting that, the day before, a work of Pierson's had been sold for more than twice its reserve price.

Where there's money there's usually trouble, Tim always said.

His thoughts were interrupted by the sound of his alarm going off. It was time to go and get Jimmy.

He was standing outside the pub, not leaning against a wall or slouching but standing straight and still. When he climbed into the car Mac noticed that he had no bag with him.

'No tools, Jimmy?'

Jimmy smiled.

'Only the one between my ears. Hopefully we'll have no need for tools today. The best way to get into any safe is to find the code. We should try that first. Anyway, if I do have to crack it, I'll need a good look at it first.'

Mac took his word for it. He knew that, when it came to safes, Jimmy knew what he was talking about.

The house in St. Ippolyts was large and rambling. The central part was very old and, over the centuries, bits and pieces seemed to have been added on at random.

A woman in her sixties opened the door. Her grey hair was neatly cut and she was elegantly dressed in black trousers and a white blouse. Mac noticed that she had very fine, high cheekbones.

'Mrs. Symonds?' Mac asked.

He gave her his card. She looked a bit puzzled.

'I'm sorry but I wasn't expecting anyone,' she replied.

'Didn't Mrs. Lynn tell you that I was coming?' Mac said. 'She's hired me to open her father's safe.'

'No, she didn't but, then again, I'm not too surprised. Everything is so up in the air at the moment. Now that I think of it, I do remember her mentioning that she needed to get the safe opened but I thought that she was going to leave it until she got back from Devon. You'd better come in then,' she said holding the door open for him and Jimmy.

They followed her through a short maze of corridors and up some stairs. They found themselves in a long room that had windows all down the side and in the roof. Paintings lay piled on one another and one half-finished one stood on an easel.

She noticed Mac looking at the painting.

'He hadn't painted for quite a while, the dementia,' she explained. 'But in the months before he died it all came back to him. He couldn't remember what had happened an hour ago but he could remember his time in New York and so he painted that.'

Mac looked at one that was propped up against a wall. It was a street scene. It was night and a young woman, a prostitute possibly, stood on a street corner while behind her the traffic, big old American cars, swept by. Her face caught the light and Mac thought he could sense a quite chilling sort of blank despair in her

129

expression. Mac had no idea if it was any good but it was definitely very powerful.

'Is this one of his recent works?' Mac asked.

'Yes, he did that the week before he died.'

'I'd guess that Mr. Pierson's works being so valuable that they'd all be on some sort of inventory. Is that right?'

'Yes, except for these later ones of course,' she replied. 'I was just happy to see him painting again. Tom could be a right sod at times but, when he was painting, he was like an angel.'

She smiled when she said this. Mac suspected that there was more to her relationship with the painter than just being an employee. He also had a good idea that the paintings Danielle had stolen must have been some of these more recent ones. If they weren't on the inventory then who would know that they even existed?

They followed the housekeeper to a door at the end of the long studio. She held it open for them.

'There it is,' she said as she pointed to the corner of the room. 'Can I get you anything?'

Mac shook his head.

'Don't go too far away though,' Jimmy said. 'We might need some information.'

'Just shout and I'll come,' she said. 'That's what I used to do for him.'

She smiled a sad smile and left them to it.

Mac noticed that a look of wonder had grown on Jimmy's face as he gazed at the large safe that took up a whole corner of the office.

'My God, it's a Chatwood and an old one at that! I never thought I'd get to see one of these.'

He ran his hand lightly along one of its edges as though he was caressing the steel box.

'What's so special about it?' Mac asked.

He was quite curious.

Jimmy smiled the first smile since they'd met.

'They produced one of the first safes that couldn't be drilled through, two half inch steel plates with a layer of molten steel and manganese in between. I really hope I don't have to crack this one, it's a beauty. The combination lock was probably fitted later.'

'So, what do we have to do first?' Mac asked.

'Perhaps nothing. The key's in the lock so let's just check that it isn't open. You'd be amazed how often I've found safes left unlocked.'

He tried the door. It didn't open.

'It was worth a try. So, as it's got a Mark IV Manifoil combination lock fitted, we need to search the room for the code. If he had dementia it's highly likely he would have written it down somewhere.'

'What would the code look like?' Mac asked. 'Six digits like in the films?'

Jimmy smiled.

'It could be if they're all over ten. There are only four numbers for this one and the last one is always zero so, in reality, we only need three. However, we have from one to ninety-nine so there's quite a choice.'

Mac rummaged around the office and passed everything with a number on to Jimmy. After an hour they'd tried everything and the safe was still locked.

'Time to shout,' Jimmy said. He went into the studio and shouted, 'Mrs. Symonds!'

A couple of minutes later she appeared. She looked at the shut safe.

'No luck yet?' she asked.

'No,' Jimmy replied. 'It doesn't look like he's written it down anywhere so it must be something memorable, something he's not likely to forget. I'd like you to write down all the important dates you can think of, birthdays, anniversaries, deaths, everything. Can you?

She thought for a moment.

'I'm pretty sure I can remember most of them.'

She spoke as she wrote.

'That's Tom's, Cathy's and Dan's birthdays and then there's Ella's birthday. She was Cathy and Dan's mother. They were married on this date and this was the date she died. Let's think...'

She sucked the end of the biro.

'Oh yes this was an important date, the date of his first exhibition.'

'You've forgotten one,' Mac said. 'What about your birthday?'

She smiled and shook her head.

'I'll put it down if you like but Tom never could remember my birthday.'

She wrote it down and then left them to it.

Mac watched silently as Jimmy tried all of the numbers backwards and forwards. It took him quite some time as the dial had to be turned five times clockwise for the first number then four turns anti-clockwise for the second number then three clockwise and two anti-clockwise for the last two.

'It's not any of these,' Jimmy stated after he'd tried the last one.

'So, what else might the code be?' Mac asked.

'Well, dates are usually the most popular but it could be anything really. It's usually something personal, something that could never be forgotten. If it's some-thing like his locker number at school then we're sunk.'

Mac had a little niggling thought at the back of his head. It was something Mrs. Symonds had said, what was it? Yes, he had it.

Jimmy had a puzzled expression on his face as he watched Mac count on his fingers.

'Try 4-1-14,' Mac said.

Jimmy did. He smiled again as the door came easily open.

'How did you get that?' he asked.

132

'It was something Mrs. Symonds said. Tom Pierson's daughters are called Catherine and Danielle but she called them Cathy and Dan. I knew that Danielle was her father's favourite so...'

'That's very clever, Mr. Maguire.'

'Anyway, here you go Jimmy. I'd have never gotten anywhere near it without you.'

Mac took the cheque for five hundred pounds he'd written our earlier from his pocket and gave it to Jimmy. He also gave him twenty pounds for a taxi home.

'Thanks, this really helps,' Jimmy said.

'Oh, before you go there's a question that I've been dying to ask you.'

'What's that?'

'That last robbery you carried out, the one where you got caught, how come they never found a note?'

'The 'You have been taxed' note, you mean?'

Mac nodded.

'I managed to shred it,' Jimmy replied.

'But they checked the shredder and found nothing.'

'Well, as the man I was robbing was a guest of the country as it were, I thought that I'd be kind. I got it translated into Arabic.'

Mac laughed out loud.

They shook hands and, Jimmy being Jimmy, he left without saying any more.

Mac took a look inside the safe. There were a few slim manila folders and a large plastic wallet so crammed with documents that it couldn't be shut properly.

He decided not to shout for Mrs. Symonds and went looking for her instead. He carried the folders awkwardly under one arm. As he passed through the lounge, he saw a framed photo of the two sisters on the wall. They were very alike except that one of them had blonde hair. For some reason Mac stopped and looked very hard at the photo. He wasn't sure exactly why.

133

'The blonde one is Danielle,' Mrs. Symonds said from behind him. 'It isn't her natural colour but she always wanted to be different to her sister. She said that they looked too much alike.'

Without taking his gaze from the photo he asked, 'What's Danielle really like?'

He could feel her hesitation even though he couldn't see her.

'She can be good fun but, I don't know, how can two sisters born less than a year apart be so different? Cathy's very dependable, a hard worker and Dan's well....Dan.'

'Tell me more,' Mac said.

'She was always wild, even as a child. If you asked her to do something then she'd do the opposite. Only Ella could manage her. After her mother died, she was uncontrollable. I think she blamed her father for Ella's death. She died in childbirth, the child, another daughter, died too. I don't think Danielle ever got over it.'

'I'd be really grateful if you could give me a carrier bag or something,' Mac asked. 'It's going to be a bit awkward carrying these and using a crutch.'

She returned with a large plastic bag from Harrods.

'Well, I suppose we should check with Mrs. Lynn before I take these off the premises.'

'I'm afraid that won't possible,' she said.

'Why is that?'

'She's staying at the family hideaway in Devon. It's right out on the wilds and you have to drive five miles to get any sort of signal on your phone.'

'Don't they have a landline?' Mac asked.

'They never had one put in. Tom liked the scenery and the isolation. He did a lot of landscapes down there and he always said that it was the one place he could work and be certain of no interruptions. Cathy loves it there too so I wasn't surprised when she said she was going down for a few days. Despite their differences, her father's death has really hit her hard.'

'Yes, she said something about liking the walking there,' Mac said.

'Well, she's different to Danielle in that too, she loves the outdoors. She met her husband Oggy when she was out fell walking. She did well falling for him, he's a really nice man. Anyway, it would probably be best if you leave it until after eight to phone her. They sometimes go to the pub around that time to eat and you can just about get a signal there.'

'She obviously forgot to tell me that. Anyway, are you sure that you're okay with me taking these away?' Mac asked just to make sure.

'It's okay. You look trustworthy enough to me plus I did check you out on the internet, DCS Maguire,' she replied with a smile.

He decided to follow her advice. He phoned Tim and said he'd meet him sometime after eight in the Magnets.

He had a couple of hours to kill so he went home and decided to try and get the documents in some sort of order for when he handed them over. The ones in the plastic wallet had all been scrunched up. Of course, that meant he'd have to look at them but he was curious and Mrs. Lynn didn't say he couldn't.

Even a quick look supplied him with more than enough evidence to put Danielle Pierson in jail. There were pages of signatures all of 'Thomas B. Pierson'. Mac guessed that this was Danielle practising her father's signature. There were bank statements from her father's and from her own bank account showing money coming and going. The amounts matched precisely. She also had several very large credits recently, probably from the sale of the paintings as well as evidence that she had been busy the month before buying real estate in Spain. As she had no job or other means of support these trans-actions could only mean one thing. She'd been robbing her father blind. Mac sighed and wondered what Mr. Pierson had done to deserve it.

He suddenly felt a sort of dissonance. There was something wrong and he was fairly sure that it was something that he'd heard or seen today. What on earth was it though?

He sat back and closed his eyes and tried to relax. He went back through the events of the day in his mind. It took him a while to realise that it was something that Mrs. Symonds had said that had caused his unease. Now, why on earth would she have said that?

For some reason the image of the two sisters kept popping into his head. There was something about it, something that he couldn't quite put his finger on. He made himself relax again and brought the photograph back into his mind. Then he thought of Catherine Lynn and made a mental snap shot of her as she sat crying outside the Magnets. He went back to the image of the two sisters.

He suddenly sat upright. He had it!

He thought back through all of the events around the Pierson case and, as astonishing as his discovery was, he found that it all suddenly made sense. He rang Tim and cancelled the pub, promising him a really fantastic story for the next time they met. He drove straight back to St. Ippolyts.

Mrs. Symonds was surprised to see him return so quickly.

Mac dispensed with any pleasantries.

'You said something earlier, something about how Cathy met her husband. Can you say it again?'

She thought for a moment.

'I said something about her finding a really nice man...'

Mac interrupted her.

'You said that they met walking?'

'Yes, fell walking.'

'Where?' Mac asked, almost holding his breath.

'Cumbria, that's where the fells are, aren't they?'

Yes, that's exactly where they are, Mac thought.

'Are you sure?' he asked.

'Yes of course, hang on a minute.'

A few minutes later she returned with a photo album. She leaved through the pages and then showed Mac a photo. It showed Cathy in walking gear. She was standing next to a young man with a beard and, in the background, there was a wooden way sign pointing to the left that said 'Cumbria Way'.

'Can you show me the picture of Cathy and Dan again?' Mac asked.

She led him down a short corridor and around a corner into the lounge. She looked mystified as he studied the photo carefully. He thought he could see it but he couldn't be sure.

'Have you got a larger photo of them both?'

'Yes, there's one upstairs,' she replied. 'Follow me.'

She led Mac up some stairs to the master bedroom. Over the bed there was a painting of a nude woman on a couch. There was something very familiar about her.

'That's you, isn't it?' Mac exclaimed in some surprise.

'Yes,' she replied with some pride. 'I used to sit for him, that's how Tom and I first got to know each other. He must have done thirty or forty paintings of me over the years. He used to joke and call me his muse.'

'You were a very beautiful woman,' Mac said.

'Thanks, it's just a shame that it doesn't last. After my husband died Tom suggested that I come and work for him and here I still am some twenty years on.'

'Were you and Tom close?' Mac asked as much out of curiosity as anything else.

'Yes, we were very good friends.' She looked at the large bed in front of them. 'After his wife died, I used to share his bed sometimes but it was more out of companionship if you know what I mean. If you acccpted the fact that the painting always came first with him then he was quite easy to get on with. I really miss him.'

A tear made its way down her cheek and Mac was again reminded of the icon.

'Anyway, here's the photo,' she said as she brushed the tear away.

She pointed to the wall.

This photo was much larger than the other one and had a better resolution. Mac examined it carefully and it confirmed what he thought he'd saw in the smaller one. This changed everything.

He decided that he had to phone Catherine Lynn that minute. He had news that couldn't wait.

He'd found something that had turned the case totally on its head.

Chapter Fourteen

Saturday – One day to Easter

He'd arranged to meet her at his office at ten thirty. He'd contacted Toni Woodgate the evening before and told her everything. The meeting was mostly her idea.

She came through the door right on time. She was wearing the same outfit as the last time they met.

'So, you managed to open the safe,' Mrs. Lynn stated with a smile. 'Well done!'

'Well, it wasn't me but the person I employed for the job who you should thank,' Mac replied. 'You owe me five hundred pounds for that by the way.'

She pulled a cheque book out of her handbag and signed her name with a flourish.

'So, I take it that you have the files?' she asked looking about the room for some evidence of them.

'Oh yes. I've got the files and a whole lot more besides.'

Mac made no move to retrieve the files or do anything else. He sat very still and looked straight at her. She seemed to detect that something wasn't right but she persevered anyway.

'Good. If you let me have them, then I'll be on my way.'

'Aren't you interested in how we cracked the code for the safe? You should be,' Mac stated.

'I suppose, if you insist…' she said with some reluctance.

'It was your nickname. I'm surprised you didn't try that as you were his favourite.'

Her face reddened but she kept up the pretence.

'I have no idea what you mean Mr. Maguire,' she protested.

'It was 4-1-14 or D-A-N if you count the letters in the alphabet. Simple really, your father knew that he was losing his mind so he used a code that he'd never forget, the name of his favourite child.'

She was visibly pulling herself together. Mac was quite impressed.

'My sister's nickname you mean,' she said. 'That's all very interesting but if you could let me have the files then I'll be off.'

'I can't do that,' Mac bluntly stated.

'What do you mean you can't do that?' she asked getting visibly agitated. 'You do have them, don't you?'

'Not any more. They're somewhere else, Danielle.'

He watched her closely as the realisation finally dawned on her that she had been found out. Mac was interested to see her body shape change and even the shape of her face. It was someone much harder that looked out at Mac now.

'So, you know. Might I ask how?' she said as she pulled out a cigarette and lit it.

'It was a really good idea but, like most amateurs, you over-egged it. A real professional would have kept it as simple as possible but you just couldn't help yourself, could you?'

'I've no idea what you mean,' she replied.

Mac could see that she didn't.

'That little side show that you put on outside the pub, you blubbing your eyes out because of the news about your horrible sister.'

'What of it? I thought that I was quite good,' she said with a self-satisfied smile.

'You were but you showed me the wrong side of your face. There's a tiny dimple on the right side of your face. You were only a couple of feet away and I noticed it when I saw you outside the pub. I noticed it again when I saw a photo of you and your sister at your father's house, the one where your hair is dyed blonde. Catherine doesn't have a dimple. Not only that but Cathy met her husband in Cumbria not Wales and that was the slip that really put me on the scent as it were. It's not something a woman would forget.'

'I knew I'd got that wrong the minute I'd said it. Oh well, how very observant of you, Mr. Maguire. So, I'm found out, oh well, it was worth a try. I'll have to grovel to Cathy of course but she'll forgive me, she always does. I suppose I'll just have to pay her back out of my half of the inheritance.'

She smiled. Mac looked at her with some wonder.

'What's your sister got to do with any of this?' he asked.

She took a big drag from her cigarette and blew the smoke in Mac's direction.

'Well, I'd have thought that she'd have to press charges or something,' she said as she looked for an ash tray.

She gave up and stubbed her cigarette out on Mac's desk.

Mac gave her a smile and it seemed to unsettle her somewhat.

'No, it doesn't quite work like that. You've stolen sums of money from your father, who was a vulnerable adult, as well as paintings probably worth well over a million pounds. It's all there in the files in black and white. You've also corrupted a solicitor, by the way he's in the local police station as we speak, singing his heart out I dare say.'

She laughed.

'He can sing away. Poor little beige man, no-one will take his word against mine. I'll say that he forced me, threatened me with violence,' she said making a sad face and fluttering her eyelids.

Mac was interested in finding out how she'd gotten around the solicitor.

'So, how did you get Barry Acourt on your side?'

'Oh, that was the easy bit. I made some eyes at him, let him take me to bed a few times and the poor thing thought he was in love.'

Mac really didn't like the woman sitting in front of him. He'd met her sister the night before and she was so totally different.

'I must admit that I didn't appreciate you using me as your cat's paw in all this either. Anyway, I'll take some comfort from the fact that you'll be spending the next few years in jail.'

The word 'jail' seemed to shock her. Her face turned pale. She took a few minutes to think.

'So, what happens now?' she asked.

'The police don't need your sister's permission to press charges when there is clear evidence of a crime having been committed. By the way, that's where the files are now, in the local police station.'

'Half the money and the paintings were mine anyway,' she protested.

'Wrong again,' Mac said. 'I found something else in that safe, a new will, one that superseded the one your boyfriend had in his safe. Your father left all his paintings to the County Council on the proviso that they built a museum to house them. That includes the ones you made off with. The museum's apparently already half built. So, in reality, you've been robbing the good people of Hertfordshire blind and not your sister. It will be really interesting to see what the judge thinks of that.'

'I'm sure the will should be easy enough to overturn. I mean his poor mind had gone, hadn't it?'

She looked quite confident about the fact.

'No, it hadn't, at least not according to his doctor who signed the will as a witness and the dementia expert who was the other witness. He had it done by another firm around the same time he gave you and your boyfriend's firm the legal power of attorney. I dare say he didn't want to upset you when you were the one who was going to be looking after him.'

'The bastard!' she exclaimed with passion. 'I was counting on those paintings.'

'You may well have been but I'm afraid that you'll have other concerns now, like trying to keep yourself out of prison.'

She looked levelly at Mac.

'I'm not afraid. I don't think it will come to that but, if it does, I'll manage it. I always do. I'll turn up dressed like a little schoolgirl, no make-up and the skirt a bit high to give the men on the jury just a little glimpse of thigh. I'll boo-hoo all the way through the trial...'

She was smiling as the tears rolled down her cheeks.

'I can cry to order,' she said. 'I'll claim that I was sexually assaulted by my father, he raped me again and again and, being traumatised, I sought revenge the only way I could. I'll make myself the real victim in all this.'

She smiled broadly at Mac.

'And did he assault you?'

'No of course not. He was an old darling but they won't know that will they?'

She smiled again.

She was even more despicable that Mac had expected.

'Oh yes they will! I'm sorry Toni but I hope you've got what you wanted because I've had quite enough of this,' Mac exclaimed.

Danielle looked behind her and then looked really puzzled.

'Who's Tony?' Danielle asked.

Mac's phone rang. He had a message. He showed it to Danielle.

It read, 'More than enough. We're on our way in. Thanks, Toni.'

It took a minute or so before the penny dropped.

'You've not been recording this, have you? I thought they only did things like that in films.'

For the first time she looked scared.

'Every word,' Mac confirmed. 'Toni, or rather I should say Detective Sergeant Antonia Woodgate, is a good copper, a bit of a stickler really. So, when I took her the

143

evidence of your crimes, she suggested that we record this interview to get even more evidence if possible. I must admit she was spot on. You've given us absolutely everything that we could have wanted.'

She stood up so abruptly she knocked the chair over.

'You bastard!' she screeched at the top of her voice. 'I won't forget this!'

'God, how unoriginal you are!' Mac said. 'I've heard those words from every low life I've ever arrested and I've arrested quite a few. I'm afraid that you're getting boring now.'

Right on cue Toni Woodgate and two burly uniformed officers entered the office.

He still could hear Danielle screaming 'Bastard' as they took her down the hallway.

'Good work, Mac,' Toni said.

'Even better work from you though, I'm impressed. You were so right about the wire. If she'd done as she'd said and claimed sexual abuse who knows what might have happened. She'd have certainly ruined her father's reputation and she might have even got away with it. Well, she can't do that now, can she?'

'No, she can't,' Toni said. 'Thanks to you it's all neatly wrapped up with a big pink bow on the top. I'd better get back and get to work. I've got lots of charges to prepare.'

She shook hands with Mac and left.

And that was that. Two cases done and dusted and it was still only Saturday.

Mac sat in the quiet of the office for a few minutes. It was only eleven and Tim wouldn't be finished at the shop until five. He thought of the two cases. Both involved the tears of a woman and false tears at that. Danielle Pierson's tears had been false and treacherous and, while the teardrop on the icon's face may not have been real, there was something incredibly truthful about it, something very human. He pictured the icon again in his mind and wondered what would happen when old Nikos revealed it to the world.

He sighed and decided that he might as well get some shopping in and then go home and wait for five o'clock.

He put the bags of shopping on the mat and opened his front door. He stood very still. He'd been expecting silence but there were sounds coming from the kitchen. He left the bags in the hall and tip-toed towards the kitchen. The radio was on and he could smell coffee.

He threw open the door. A figure turned and looked at him with surprise.

'Dad! I didn't hear you come in.'

'Bridget, what a surprise!' he said as he gave her a big hug. 'I take it that coffee's nearly ready then?'

It was. After she'd helped him put the shopping away, they both sat down in the living room. Mac couldn't get the smile off his face.

'It's so good to see you,' he said.

She leaned over and gave his hand a squeeze.

'And you. I just wish I could get over more often.'

'So, what brings you here today? I mean I know you want to see me but...oh well you know what I mean.'

'Yes, living and working in London does make things a bit difficult sometimes. I just wish I could visit more often,' she said. 'To be honest I wasn't planning on coming today, I actually managed to get Easter off and I was going to spend a couple of days with Tommy.'

'I take it that a case came up?' Mac asked.

He couldn't help smiling though. Tommy's loss was certainly his gain.

'Unfortunately, yes, but I was coming to see you tomorrow anyway, we both were. Come and have a look.'

She took him to the fridge and showed him a truly massive leg of lamb.

'We were going to do that for you and Tim tomorrow, at least that was the plan,' she said with a sigh.

Mac could see that his daughter wasn't happy about something. He thought he knew what.

'Are you finding the going with Tommy a bit tough?' he asked. 'It's hard being with a policeman. You can try and plan ahead but you never know what's going to come up at the last minute. You know I often wonder if your mother ever regretted marrying me...'

Bridget cut him short.

'No dad, no she didn't,' she said with absolute certainty.

'How can you be so sure of that?'

'She told me a couple of weeks before she died. She said that she'd loved her life and the only thing she regretted was not having a little longer to spend with you and me.'

Mac's eyes brimmed with tears.

'That sounds like your mother alright but what about you? It must have been hard having me as a father, all those school plays I missed.'

'If I'm honest it was hard at times,' Bridget said. 'I remember we did a musical once when I was at primary school. We'd rehearsed for weeks and I so wanted you to see me in my costume. I was a star if I remember right. I had my own song and everything. Of course, you couldn't make it and I got a bit upset as all the other fathers were there. Later that night, Mum let me stay up late. I remember that we drank hot chocolate and cuddled up together on the sofa. We saw you on the news giving a press conference about some murderer that you'd caught. You know what Mom said to me?'

Mac shook his head.

'She told me that your job was to go out into the world and catch all the bad men that were out there so that everyone else could sleep safely in their beds at night. It was our job, mine and hers, to help you to do that. I felt like a very important nine year old after she said that. She let me stay up until you came in so I could

146

tell you how proud I was of you and tell you what a success I'd been in the musical too, of course.'

The tears started streaming down Mac's face.

'I remember,' he said.

She hugged him and said, 'I'm sorry Dad, have I made you sad?'

'No, no you haven't,' he said as he wiped the tears away. 'It used to be that any thought of your mother would do that but now, when I remember her, I just thank God that she was in my life.'

'Me too.'

Mac got a tissue, blew his nose and pulled himself together.

'You have got something on your mind though, haven't you?' he asked.

She grimaced.

'Yes, I've got a decision to make, possibly two.'

'Do you want to talk about it?'

'If you don't mind. I've been offered a job at the Lister Hospital in Stevenage. It's only about the same money but it's a sort of promotion, I suppose. It will mean more responsibility but also the chance to try out some new ideas.'

'So?'

'I must admit that I don't enjoy living in London that much but I do like working at the Royal Free. It's exciting and it makes me feel like I'm at the centre of things.'

Mac's heart leapt at the possibility of his daughter living so close to home but he tried to keep a straight face. He didn't want to influence her decision.

'Well, only you can make that call,' he said. 'You said that you had two decisions to make?'

Bridget pulled another face.

'I'm not quite so certain about this one but Tommy's been looking for a flat in Letchworth and I've been helping him.'

Tommy Nugent was a Detective Constable working out of Luton police station. He'd worked with Mac on his first case and Mac liked him a lot. He was quite glad when he'd heard that he and his daughter had started going out together. Mac was puzzled at Tommy wanting to move to Letchworth though.

'Why? It would be a bit far for him to go to work in Luton every day. Why would he be looking here?'

'Because he's going to be working out of Letchworth police station in a month or so,' Bridget replied. 'After that case you worked on in Luton Dan Carter, his boss, has been promoted. He's a Detective Superintendent now and they've put him in charge of a new Major Crime Unit covering the three counties. There'll be policemen in the unit from the Bedfordshire and Cambridgeshire forces as well as Hertfordshire, so he asked Tommy if he'd be interested in joining him.'

'I'll bet that Tommy nearly bit his hand off, didn't he?' Mac said.

'Something like that. Anyway, while we were looking at this particular flat, a bit large for a single man I thought, I just let the thought slip out that I might, sort of, see myself living there.'

She gave her father a shame faced look.

'What did he say?' Mac asked.

'Nothing but he did give me this very meaningful look.'

'Is it getting that serious?' he asked. 'You've only known each other for three months or so.'

'How long was it before you and Mom knew?'

'I asked her to marry me four weeks to the day after we first met.'

'What did she say?' Bridget asked.

'Nothing at first then, a week later, she asked me who I thought we should invite on my side and that was that. We were married four months later, the longest four months of my life I may add. I think it's so much better these days, you know moving in together and seeing how it goes first.'

His daughter looked very thoughtful.

'Are you worried about how you'd feel if Tommy does ask you to move in with him?' he asked.

'God no, I'm just worried he might not ask that's all. Of course, it's all tied up with the job. If he does asks me then it would be good to be working local and not going in and out of London every day but...oh I just don't know!' she said looking a bit exasperated.

'Can I suggest that you let it rest over Easter and talk it over with Tommy when you see him. The answer will come to you.'

'Thanks Dad,' she said as she gave him a hug. 'It's so nice to be home again.'

Chapter Fifteen

Easter Sunday

Mac and Bridget were up early that Sunday.

They'd arranged to meet Tim for breakfast in the Magnets and after that they were all going back to Mac's house for the day.

Bridget did most of the cooking and Mac acted as sous-chef while Tim threw in suggestions from the side lines. By four o'clock the leg of lamb was served up and even Mac had to admit that it knocked all the foot-long hotdogs in the Magnets into a big cocked hat.

After dinner they all sat on the sofa and watched a children's animated movie on the TV. He found it was surprisingly funny.

Mac turned to comment on one scene and saw Bridget's sad little face. She had tears in her eyes. He leaned over and held her hand.

'Missing Mum?'

She nodded.

'And my Easter egg. Why do people think you grow out of them?' she said grumpily.

Without another word Mac got up and went into the kitchen. He returned with the Easter egg he'd bought in the supermarket. He'd put it away on top of one of the kitchen cupboards and had almost forgotten about it.

'Now that's what I call an egg!' Tim said admiringly.

'God, it's massive. How did you know?' Bridget asked with a huge smile on her face

'I didn't, I just bought it and I'm so glad I did.'

A few minutes afterwards Mac took a sip of wine and looked around the room. His good friend Tim, who had been a rock for him to cling to when times were bad, was laughing out loud at the movie. He had a good laugh.

His beautiful daughter Bridget sat curled up with the remains of the smashed Easter egg on her lap. She was smiling and she had chocolate smeared along her top lip. She looked nine years old again.

Mac felt strange, very strange. An unexpected feeling rose up in him, one that he thought he'd never feel again.

He was happy.

Chapter Sixteen

Easter Monday
BBC TV News

'...well you might well have been wondering why we've been rushing through the news this Easter Monday evening and I can tell you that it's because we're now going to bring you a very special report from Greece, one we think that you'll really like. This report was filmed earlier by our correspondent Ben Cottinger in the town of Agiou Athiris in Central Greece.'

The scene moved from the news studio to that of a man standing outside on a street.

'I'm standing here outside what might seem a more or less normal family home in a fairly ordinary Greek town some two hundred kilometres north of Athens. However, what happened here last Saturday evening can be truly described as extraordinary and its ripples seem to have affected just about everyone in this troubled country.

This is the house of Nikos Nicolaou. He's a retired history professor and, from all reports, someone not normally given to flights of fancy. However, last Friday, after returning home from holiday, a dream woke him in the night. It was a dream so powerful that he couldn't forget it. The next morning he told his grandson, also called Nikos, all about it.

What he saw in this dream was a soldier carrying something from a burning building and then his father pointing to the wall of an attic room in the house. The first part of the dream, he said, was actually a memory of a real event, one which he thought he'd all but forgotten. In 1947 the local security forces had burnt down the church that had stood in the main square of the town. This was in retaliation for a jail break that had freed six Partisans, one of them being Mr. Nicolaou's father.

In the church there was an icon that they called 'Our Lady of Agiou Athiris'. It had been the focal point of the town's religious devotions for many centuries. Every Easter the icon would be garlanded with flowers and there would be a procession through all the parishes in the town. Of course, everyone assumed that the icon had been burnt to ashes along with everything else in the church. One resident who had witnessed the events said that the loss of the icon had broken the town's heart and that it had never really recovered from its loss.

However, Mr. Nicolaou, only nine years old at the time, had been hiding in an alleyway and he saw a soldier run through the flames and out of a door at the rear of the burning church. He was holding the icon. It had not been consigned to the flames after all. He told his mother about it but she ordered him to forget what he'd just seen and apparently that's just what he did.

In the second part of the dream, Mr. Nicolaou said that he saw his dead father standing in the attic of the house pointing towards a wall.

As I said Mr. Nicolaou, being not at all religious, might be the last man who you might think would act on such a dream but he and his grandson did just that. They tore away part of the brick wall in the attic and, to both of their surprise, they found something.

Around six o'clock he called together every member of his extended family for a meeting and that evening sixty or seventy people somehow crammed themselves inside this house. There Mr. Nicolaou recounted the story of his dream and then showed them what they had found behind the attic wall. It was Our Lady of Agiou Athiris, the icon that everyone thought had been destroyed some seventy years before.

The very oldest members of the family fell straight to their knees as they knew the icon for what it was. The younger members had never seen the real icon just an old black and white photograph that had stood in its place in the rebuilt church. All that they had left of the icon or so they'd thought.

The whole family, one by one, said a little prayer and then kissed the corner of the frame which has been the tradition in this town for centuries. Mr. Nicolaou also showed them something else that they had found with the icon, a photograph of the soldier who had saved it. He said that his father must have placed it in with the icon when he'd concealed it in the wall. He told his family that it was now their duty to return the icon to its proper place and asked if they would all help him to do it.

So, the whole Nicolaou family assembled right here on the street outside this house and then started walking that way towards the town centre. At the front of the procession the young Nikos Nicolaou held the icon aloft and old Nikos held the photograph of the soldier.

Here's what one of the neighbours, Maria Angeletou said about it–

'I was sitting outside talking to my good friend Sofia when I saw them all walking down the road towards us. I said, 'Look at those crazy Nicolaous. What are they up to now?' As they got closer, I saw what young Nikos was holding, I saw her. I knew it was her the moment I saw it. After all these years she had come back to us. I fell to my knees while they passed by and crossed myself, then Sofia and me joined them.'

And it was not just Sofia and Maria that joined the Nicolaou family. As they walked down this hill people sitting outside these bars and restaurants also joined in. The word spread by mobile phone and by the time they reached the main road here they were around three to four hundred strong. Now, as you can see, this is a fairly busy road, with two lanes of traffic going each way, but last Saturday the traffic stopped. No-one seemed to mind though, in fact it seems that many of the drivers parked up their cars and joined in the march as well.

By the time they reached the main square here they were well over five hundred strong and at least as many again were waiting for them to arrive. Some of the younger and stronger members of the family had to force their way through the crowds so they could make it to the church. Once there they were met outside the church by the priest, Father Karas, who accepted the icon from Mr. Nicolaou. It's said that neither men spoke a word as the icon was handed over. They explained afterwards that this was because they just couldn't find any words that could fully express their feelings.

The priest, with some help, climbed onto this wall and then held the icon above his head so that the ever-growing crowd could see it. He recited the 'Hail Mary' and then kissed the corner of the frame. This is what it is reported that the priest said next–

'She has come back to us. Our Lady has come back to us in this time of austerity. It is a sign.'

There was a murmuring in the crowd until in almost one voice they started shouting in unison over and over again 'Our Lady of Austerity', a name she's been known by here ever since. That night the priest insisted that the icon should rest in the quiet of the church but there would be little rest in the town. There was a procession to arrange for the next day, the first for seven decades. Even those who had no part to play in the planning of the Easter festivities didn't go to sleep. They were just happy to sit and talk over the wondrous events all through the night.

Before they put the icon to rest however a local news team got the story on film and on Easter Sunday, along with their breakfasts, most of the country watched the story of the miraculous return of 'Our Lady of Austerity'. It hit home with a lot of Greeks, so much so that the procession, which used to take two hours at most, took over six as it attracted people from all over Greece. People like twenty nine year old Ekaterina who had this to say –

'We live about eighty kilometres away from Agiou Athiris but when we heard about the icon on the news my husband and I got in our car and drove straight here. We're not so religious but times have been very hard for us and I suppose that we just needed some hope. We found it here, in her sad face and in the smiles all around us. I can't remember the last time I felt this happy. We feel that we have some hope again.'

So, another story about austerity from Greece, I suppose, but one that is thankfully a bit different. As one man told me after seeing the icon for himself, 'When I saw the light reflecting from the painting, I thought that this indeed is the light at the end of the tunnel being switched on again for all Greece.'

(Newsreader) 'Well that was filmed some hours ago but we can now go back to Ben who's still in the main square in Agiou Athiris. Ben what's been happening?'

'Well, it's not far off midnight here but as you can see the square is still packed with people. First though I'd like to show you a little clip, a clip that's gone viral all over the world via the internet. Here you can see a man examining the icon. He's one of the world's leading experts on icons from this period and he was sent here by the government to check that it was genuine. He examined the icon for about half an hour. The video then shows him packing his tools away in a bag. Everyone knew the icon was genuine when he knelt down in front of the icon and kissed the corner of the frame. He then stood up and, with a huge grin on his face, he said, 'She is so beautiful.' There's no need to guess what all the headlines are going to be tomorrow. Anyway, once he'd said that a cheer went from the church to the crowd outside and the whole town erupted. The Prime Minister visited an hour later and he called it 'a sure sign that as a nation we can beat austerity.'

People are still flooding into the town from all over the country. I spoke to the man who owns the hotel over there in the corner of the square and he said that normally they would be lucky to be a quarter full. A couple of hours ago he said that the earliest you could get a room would be near Christmas and it's probably next year by now. He said that he's already had to take on four times as many staff as normal to cope with the influx of visitors. The 'Miracle of Agiou Athiris', as they're calling it, has really hit a nerve in the Greek public's imagination and, here at least, austerity had ended as this town has been turned into something of a national shrine.

Before I go, we've just discovered that there's a surprising connection with Britain. The photograph of the soldier who rescued the icon from the burning church has been identified as that of a Captain Harry Llewellyn-fforbes of the Hertfordshire Regiment. He led a small unit that fought with the Partisans in the Second World War. They call him 'Captain Harry' here and he's already become something of a saint in the town's eyes.'

(Newsreader) 'Thanks for that Ben. A feel-good story from Greece at last. Now I wish that I could say the same about the weather but I'm afraid that it's going to be raining pretty much everywhere...'

Four weeks later

Mac was once again putting his shopping into the boot of the old Almera at the supermarket. He'd just driven out of the car park onto Broadway when he noticed a familiar figure sitting on one of the benches. He parked as close as he could and walked over.

He sat down next to the man. He was so deep in thought that he didn't even glance in his direction.

'Hello Monty,' Mac said. 'Nice day, isn't it?'

The old man awoke as if from a dream.

'Oh, it's you Mac!' he said. He smiled broadly and offered his hand. 'I'm sorry but I was miles away.'

'I'd guess about two thousand miles away,' Mac said as he shook his hand.

Monty laughed.

'Yes, you're spot on there. I must say that it all takes a bit of thinking about.'

'When did you get back?'

'Just three days ago. I'm still in shock though, I think.'

'I saw you on the news,' Mac said.

'Yes, everyone's said that. My little visit seems to have created quite a splash.'

'What was it like?' Mac asked.

Monty looked up the sky before answering.

'It was like nothing I've ever experienced before. You know I used to see those pop star chappies on the TV and wondered what it must be like. Crowds everywhere you go and all that. I finally got a taste of it and at my age too. Helena and I had no idea what we were letting ourselves in for when we booked the flights. That's all we had to do as she'd been in contact with young Nikos and he arranged the hotel and everything else.'

Mac would have bet that she'd more than willingly volunteered for that job.

'We should have known something was up when we mysteriously got upgraded to first class and then had the money for the flights refunded. We definitely should have twigged when the pilot and co-pilot made a point of coming out and shaking our hands before we took off. They announced it over the tannoy you know, 'the son of Captain Harry is on board' they said. A cheer went up. I thought they were all watching football or something and someone had scored a goal.

Then we were met at the airport by both young and old Nikos. We followed them into what I thought would be the arrivals area when old Nikos apologised and said that it couldn't be avoided. We walked into a huge room full of journalists and photographers. It was a press conference just for me and Helena. They fired questions at us for fifteen minutes or so but they were all very nice.'

'Yes, I saw a bit of it. I thought you were very good. You looked quite calm.'

Monty smiled.

'I was quaking in my boots I can tell you. Well, luckily, they managed to smuggle us out of the airport and young Nikos drove us to Agiou Athiris. I sat in the back with old Nikos. We talked non-stop, he's a most interesting man you know. I couldn't help noticing that Helena and young Nikos weren't talking so much but they were looking at each other a lot which I thought was a bit strange.

Anyway, we walked into the hotel through the back entrance and they were all there to meet us. Not just the staff but all the guests too. They clapped and cheered and I just didn't know what to make of it. I tried to pay for our rooms but the owner looked offended and said that, 'The son of Captain Harry will never spend a cent while he is in my hotel.'

I was still wondering what was happening when we went to the restaurant next door for something to eat. It was absolutely packed but young Nikos had a word with the owner and like magic a table was produced and people were moved to make way. When we sat down the owner announced who we were to the whole room. They all stood up and clapped. Later, after we'd finished eating, loads of them asked to have their photo taken with us. It was all very strange.

The day after old Nikos had arranged for us to visit the icon. We only had to walk across the square but, with all the people and the photographers, it took us quite a while. It was quiet in the church, I didn't realise it but there'd been thousands of people visiting the icon every day, so many that all they could do was walk past it and quickly look at it. They gave us five minutes alone with her which was a real honour.

God knows I thought she was beautiful the first time I saw her but there, in the proper setting, I thought her beyond beauty, beyond this world even. I prayed and kissed the corner of the frame. Below her they'd put the photo of my father, so that everyone who visits will know who saved her, so the priest said. I must admit I cried when I saw that.'

Mac could see the tears form in his eyes as he said this.

'They were all very good and laid on loads of things for us to do while we were there but I'm afraid that I had to do most of them by myself.'

'Why was that?' Mac asked.

'There were lots of sick people turning up who needed medical help and the local hospital had set up a clinic in a disused shop near the church,' Monty replied. 'Young Nikos, being a good sort, was helping them out. As soon as she heard, Helena volunteered as well. I hardly saw her after that. I noticed that the day before I left, she and young Nikos were walking hand in hand. I don't know what had happened between them but it was obvious to everyone that they were a couple now. She's still there with him now. She's working very hard because there's so many people to look after but I must admit that I've never seen her so happy.'

Monty took out his phone and gave it to Mac.

'She sent me this yesterday.'

Mac looked at the photo. Helena and young Nikos were in white doctor's coats with T shirts and shorts on underneath. They both had a sheen of sweat on their faces. He had his right hand resting on her shoulder while her left arm was around his waist. They weren't looking at the camera but at each other, looking right into each other's eyes as only lovers can do. They were both smiling.

'Mind you she could do far worse,' Monty said as he took back the phone. 'I really like young Nikos a lot but, if I'm honest, it's hard losing Helena. It was so nice having her around the house.'

Mac gave it some thought.

'Well, it might not be so bad.'

'How do you mean?' Monty asked.

'Nikos is technically on sabbatical leave so, in time, he might carry on his studies here at the Medical School. If that's the case then they'll both be looking for somewhere to stay and your house is so big.'

'Yes, I hadn't thought of that,' Monty said with a smile.

'And if they do decide to settle in Greece just think of how nice and warm it is there when the snow is on the ground over here. It would be really good to have somewhere like that to go for a nice long holiday, now wouldn't it?'

Monty laughed out loud.

'You've really cheered me up Mac. I'm so glad we bumped into each other today,'

As Mac drove home, he thought about the two cases. The one that had looked so sinister at first but had turned out to be anything but and the other, the one that had looked so straight forward, had proved to be a cruel deception from start to finish.

What linked them both were tears. A woman's tears were an incredibly powerful thing, Mac thought. He remembered how he'd made Nora cry once or twice and the regrets still stung him now as he thought about it. He also remembered the making up afterwards.

He thought about the making up all the way home.

THE END

I hope you enjoyed this story. If you have then please leave a review and let me know what you think.

Also in the Mac Maguire detective series

The Body in the Boot

The Dead Squirrel

The Blackness

23 Cold Cases

Two Dogs

The Match of the Day Murders

The Chancer

The Tiger's Back

The Eight Bench Walk

https://patrickcwalshauthor.wordpress.com/

Made in the USA
Middletown, DE
15 February 2021